PUF

WEB OF LIES

Beverley Naidoo was born in South Africa and as a student became involved in resistance to apartheid. She began writing in exile in England and her first children's book, the award-winning *Journey to Jo'burg*, was banned in South Africa until 1991. Enormously successful elsewhere, it opened a window for many thousands of readers on to what apartheid meant for children. A sequel, *Chain of Fire*, and *No Turning Back*, about a runaway streetchild, and her short stories in *Out of Bounds* continued to explore the drama of young people's lives in her birth country. *The Other Side of Truth*, about two refugee children smuggled to London, won the Carnegie Medal in 2000. She has written picture books, poetry and plays including *The Playground*. She is also the author of *Through Whose Eyes?*, based on doctoral research into teenage responses to literature.

www.beverleynaidoo.com

WEB OF LIES

Beverley Naidoo

PUFFIN

PUFFIN BOOKS

Published by the Penguin Group
Penguin Books Ltd, 80 Strand, London WC2R 0RL, England
Penguin Group (USA), Inc., 375 Hudson Street, New York, New York 10014, USA
Penguin Books Australia Ltd, 250 Camberwell Road, Camberwell, Victoria 3124, Australia
Penguin Books Canada Ltd, 10 Alcorn Avenue, Toronto, Ontario, Canada M4V 3B2
Penguin Books India (P) Ltd, 11 Community Centre, Panchsheel Park, New Delhi – 110 017, India
Penguin Group (NZ), cnr Airborne and Rosedale Roads, Albany, Auckland 1310, New Zealand
Penguin Books (South Africa) (Pty) Ltd, 24 Sturdee Avenue, Rosebank 2196, South Africa

Penguin Books Ltd, Registered Offices: 80 Strand, London WC2R 0RL, England

www.penguin.com

First published 2004
4

Copyright © Beverley Naidoo, 2004
All rights reserved

The moral right of the author has been asserted

Set in Linotype Palatino
Typeset by Rowland Phototypesetting Ltd, Bury St Edmunds, Suffolk

Made and printed in England by Clays Ltd, St Ives plc

British Library Cataloguing in Publication Data
A CIP catalogue record for this book is available from the British Library

ISBN 0–141–31466–4

ACKNOWLEDGEMENTS

Many people have generously helped me during my research and writing. Although I have space to mention only some by name, my thanks go to them all.

Olusola Oyeleye offered me her wonderful drama workshops, unflagging interest in my fictional characters and insightful comments on the real world they inhabit. I also thank the many young people who spoke so openly and honestly. These include students at Charles Edward Brooke School, Camberwell, London, with particular thanks to Vwarhe Eguridu, Cherish Nwokike, Donna Rafferty and Monisola Britto; and students at the From Boyhood to Manhood Foundation in Peckham. I am much indebted to its director Uanu Seshmi. My thanks go to Camilla Batmanghelidjh at Kids Company and The Bosco Centre, south London; Ruth Symister and students at Whitefield Fishponds Community School, Bristol; Sharon Muiruri and members of Vita Nova, Bournemouth; Sheila Melzak, Medical Foundation for the Care of Victims of Torture; Jill Rutter, London Metropolitan University; Praveen Naidoo; Det. Chief Inspector Brooker; Jeanette Redding; Deborah Catesby; Hannah Lake and Maya Naidoo. As ever Jane Nissen and Hilary Delamere have provided unstinting support, and my husband Nandha, his patience and sustenance.

For Bisi and David

CONTENTS

The South London Echo
26th December 1995

CHILDREN REUNITED WITH HUNGER-STRIKING DAD
Home Secretary orders release of asylum-seeker

Two children who campaigned to free their father from prison were rewarded on Christmas Eve when he was released by special order of the Home Secretary. Folarin Solaja, a journalist from Nigeria, has been on hunger strike for the last two weeks at Heathlands Detention Centre. He is seeking asylum in Britain.

In Nigeria, Solaja is known for his outspoken criticism of the military dictator General Abacha. Six weeks ago his wife was shot dead by gunmen in an attack at his Lagos home. Solaja says that further death threats were made to his family. 'I was their real target. These assassins were acting on the highest orders.'

Solaja admits that his children, Sade (12) and Femi (10), were smuggled into London and that he tried to enter Britain a week later on false papers. 'I did not know where my children were and I was desperate to find them before sorting out my position.' He says he was not aware that claims for asylum have to be made immediately on arrival. 'When challenged by immigration officers, I tried to explain but I was arrested.'

Solaja says 'a miracle' reunited him with his children, who had been abandoned in London by their courier. A Refugee Adviser visiting Heathlands Detention Centre was able to identify them despite the false surname they had given to social workers.

When Nigerian officials demanded Solaja's extradition on a charge of murdering his wife, he began a hunger strike. 'They trumped up the charge to get me back. I have always fought for the truth. It pains me that we had to lie about ourselves to save our lives.'

Solaja paid tribute to his children for bringing his plight to the attention of a television news presenter. Asked about their father's release, Sade replied, 'He is our best Christmas present.'

LONDON

September 1997

CHAPTER 1

'Hi, little brother!'

The first hullabaloo left Femi pressed against the wall like a leech. The blaring siren brought a tidal wave of bodies swooping down the corridor. He glimpsed his friend Gary's sandy-brown hair bob away and disappear. By the time he could prise himself off the wall, he was alone. Late and lost.

From behind closed doors came the muffled sounds of classes settling down. He scurried along the empty corridor, trying to delve into his bag at the same time. He needed to consult his map. There was a T-junction coming up. Was Maths to the left? His heart was already pumping fast when the second hullabaloo struck. A whacking great thud . . . a raw, yelping howl . . . sudden laughter. Then a posse of older boys careered around the corner from the left, one almost tumbling over Femi. The boy swore as Femi's eyes met his. Dark black pupils in a delicate brown web. A flicker like a camera shutter. Femi didn't wait. He darted around the corner.

Deep, awful moans arose from a man crouched in the doorway of the nearest classroom. With his head drawn in like a wounded soldier, he was rocking back and forth, clutching one hand over the other. Femi gaped at the emerging tattoo of red rivulets.

The children inside the room looked strangely frozen, except for a girl and boy standing close behind the kneeling figure. First years, like Femi.

'Miss! Help, miss!' They signalled frantically at a teacher hurrying down the corridor. Noisy older students spilt out from the classroom behind her.

'Sir's fingers caught in the door, miss!' squealed the girl.

'Someone slammed it, miss!' The boy looked ashen. 'Sir was looking the other way!'

Femi stood transfixed as a crowd swirled around him to see the injured teacher.

'WHAT is going on here?' a voice thundered behind them. 'Get back to class immediately, all of you! Back to class!'

Femi had only been two days at Avon High, but already he recognized the voice of Mr Gordon, the deputy head. Flash Gordon! His sister Sade had told him the nickname. It was a joke. He was tall and broad-shouldered but he had a large pot belly and thinly spread-out grey hair. However, his voice was deep and powerful and it propelled Femi out of the combat zone, down the corridor in search of his Maths class.

'Sorry, miss, I got lost!' Femi mumbled.

Ms Hassan raised her eyebrows and placed him in an empty seat near her, nowhere near Gary or any of the others from his primary school. This was 7B's second lesson with Ms Hassan, and Femi had already seen that her tongue was even sharper than her eyebrows. Terminator eyebrows, said Gary. Femi tried to concentrate on the numbers that squeaked out from the chalk scratching the blackboard. He copied the multiplication sums into his new exercise book slowly and neatly. But when it came to filling in the answers, the pen poised above the page suffered a blockage. He began to panic, trying to think. But his brain could only conjure up a figure curled over in pain – and a pair of eyes clicking in front of him like a camera shutter. When Ms Hassan did not collect the books but said they should complete the sums for homework, he breathed more easily.

Femi slid next to Gary as they left the room. Even before Gary opened his packet of crisps, Femi was recounting his tale of blood-curdling cries and a teacher on the floor with blood spurting like a fountain from his hands. He said nothing, however, about the posse of boys in flight. Something made him hold back. Instead, he let Gary go on about the class hearing a weird faraway howl and how Ms Hassan had stopped anyone from leaving their desks.

They had been friends for a whole year now. Gary had joined the top class at Greenslades Primary. Femi had been new the year before and had slipped into being a loner. But something about Gary had appealed to him. He liked the way Gary had shrugged off comments about his Liverpool accent. His mother had brought him down to London to live with a new stepdad. There had been gossip about his real dad dying in a terrible accident, but Femi had never asked questions. He knew about not prising open a lid that was nailed down.

By lunchtime, the rumours had spread about a teacher losing a finger. There was talk of an ambulance driving into Avon school. Someone said they had seen a police car. However, apart from Gary, Femi didn't tell anyone else that he had seen the teacher rocking in agony on the floor.

They were edging nearer the canteen hatch when Femi felt a hand on his shoulder. He swung round.

'Hi, little brother! Long time no see!' The boy with the dark-brown camera eyes smiled and hustled between him and Gary. Femi bit his lip.

'Keep my brother's place, right!' the older boy ordered Gary, steering Femi away.

'There's a girl, Sade, in my class. Is she your sister?' The grip allowed no resistance but the boy's voice was soft and quite friendly.

Femi nodded, avoiding looking up.

'Yeah, you look alike but you're not as pretty as her, are you?'

Femi swallowed, his mouth dry.

'Just a joke, right! What's your name?'

Femi managed to say his name, not much louder than a whisper.

'OK, Femi. I want you to give her a message.'

So, was this just about Sade? Femi picked up courage.

'But you said she's in your class.' He couldn't hide the puzzlement.

'Girls like a bit of mystery!' laughed the boy. 'Just tell her Errol likes her and don't tell her how you know.'

'Is that you? Errol?' Femi ventured.

'No way, man! You don't know Errol Richards?'

Femi shook his head.

'Where've you been, man? You live round here and you don't know Errol Richards? You, little brother, sure got a lot to learn!'

Femi didn't want to say that he had indeed heard

the surname 'Richards'. There had been a Richards in the year above him at his primary school and he had tried to keep well clear of him. That Richards had been sent to another school, to the relief of most of the children. Femi didn't know what to say now. It would be awkward to ask if they were related. Instead, he shot a glance at the lunch queue. Gary was nearly at the front.

'I've got to –'

The older boy smiled and put his arm around Femi again.

'Well, even if you're still a bit ignorant, I like you, Femi. You'll learn fast, man. You need to, around here. You need somebody to look out for you – like Errol did for me.'

There was something the older boy wasn't saying.

'The brothers need to stick together, right?' The boy was bending over now, almost whispering. Femi felt the pressure of the hand on his shoulder. 'There's always someone wants to put us down ... make up stories ... things they didn't see with their own eyes. You know what I mean?'

Femi didn't know whether to nod or shake his head. When you can't see what is underfoot in the forest, how do you know where to step? He was being steered back towards Gary, who was calling anxiously.

'You give that message to your sister, right? You tell me what she says next time I see you, little brother!' The boy spoke loud enough for Gary to hear as he gave Femi a slight shove towards the canteen hatch.

'Is he your brother? You never said!' Gary jutted his chin out accusingly.

Femi frowned.

'Not that kind of brother. I'm hungry. Thought I was going to miss my turn.'

The canteen lady eyed him.

'Chips, please.'

Femi didn't want Gary to interrogate him. He didn't even know the older boy's name. Why did he choose Femi to talk to as a 'brother'? This wasn't just a message for Sade. The camera eyes made that clear. It was a message to him.

They headed for a table that was filling up. Two Year Seven girls were at the centre of a cluster.

'Sir had his fingers in the door. Must have broken all of 'em! It was a right slam!'

'It was only his forefinger! I saw the bit at the end hanging off.'

'Yuk! You didn't!'

'I did. It was horrible. But only for a second like, before sir grabbed it, trying to push it back!'

'Jason says he saw the fingertip fly across the room!'

There was a burst of laughter.

'Oh, disgusting! D'you mind, we're eating.'

'Did sir see who did it?'

'Nah! He was just screaming and bawling his head off!'

'Slammed the door from behind, didn't they?'

'Change the conversation, will you? I'm going to be sick!'

Flash Gordon called a special afternoon assembly after lunch. Images from the morning flooded back as the deputy head spoke about 'a very serious incident'.

He emphasized that it was a supply teacher who was involved.

'A visitor new to our school, helping us out, and this is how we welcomed him . . .'

Femi felt his stomach cramping. Being 'new' was something he knew all about.

'One finger was almost severed. The doctors are still struggling to see what they can do. If charges of assault are made, the police will . . .'

Another sharp cramp. Femi pressed his folded arms against his lower ribs.

'. . . it will be better for everyone if the matter can be handled within school. It might have started as a foolish prank with someone not thinking of the consequences. However it occurred, I want whoever is responsible to own up and do the decent thing now. Anyone else – who heard or saw anything – should come and see me as soon as possible.'

Blood rushed up to his head, making it throb. Gary poked him.

'Get up, Femi! We've already missed twenty minutes!'

Femi threw himself into the football practice in an effort to wipe out the words from assembly. But when he and Gary jostled their way out of school at home time, a new spasm of cramp gripped Femi's stomach. Flash Gordon loomed over them on the front steps. He looked grim enough to be an immigration officer! Femi wanted to tell Gary, to try to make a joke of it. But he had hardly ever spoken, not even to Gary, about their immigration trouble. When their Year Six class at Greenslades Primary had made a day-trip to France,

Femi and a new girl from Kosovo were the only two children left behind. In school, Femi had made light of it. He had pretended that he wasn't bothered about spending a day with Year Fives while Gary and the others went off on their coach and ferry. But at home he had cried himself to sleep, tasting the salt in his tears. Papa had explained that until the government accepted that they were proper refugees, they couldn't get any travel documents. Femi could leave England, but the immigration officers wouldn't let him back in! They would separate him from Papa and Sade! Where would they expect him to go? A twelve-year-old boy, who didn't even speak French, all alone in France.

Just as Gary had never spoken of what happened to his dad, Femi had said nothing about Papa being locked up when he first arrived in the country. Nor did Gary know about The Interview. In Heathlands Detention Centre, Papa had filled in a long form about why it was too dangerous for them to go home to Nigeria. He had described the police raids on their home in Lagos as well as the day the gunmen came. Femi had seen a copy of the form when Mr Nathan, their lawyer, wanted to check what the children remembered of events that Femi preferred to forget. Mr Nathan had turned over pages and pages filled with Papa's small, neat writing. Obviously the immigration officers thought Papa might be lying. That was why he had to go to The Interview. They would try to trip Papa up. Trap him. Then they would refuse him permission to stay in England. Papa and the children would be put on a plane back to Nigeria, where General Abacha and his soldiers would be waiting for them.

Papa had prepared himself like he was getting ready

for an exam. He didn't know when he would be called, and every month he had to report to the police station as an asylum-seeker. They had waited almost a year. Femi had just moved into Year Six when a letter arrived with I.N.D. printed boldly on the front. The Immigration and Nationality Directorate ordered Papa to present himself at Heathrow Airport. Only Papa was to be interviewed, not the children. It was very scary. What if the immigration officers suddenly forced Papa on to a plane – or took him back into prison? On the day of The Interview, Femi kept expecting his head teacher to appear at the classroom door. She would call him out to give him the bad news.

By home time, however, there had been no news. He and Sade had run all the way back to their flat. It was empty. They had waited, fearing the worst. Papa arrived in the evening. He looked wrung out.

I told them everything – the whole truth. We should be all right.

Femi knew that he was just trying to reassure them. None of the immigration officers at the Asylum Screening Unit had made him feel 'all right'. But Papa insisted that their case was very strong and they must continue to be patient.

They had waited and waited. Every time Mr Nathan tried to find out what was happening, he was told that a decision had not yet been made. When another letter finally arrived with I.N.D. on the envelope, Femi and his sister had been on tenterhooks. They watched as Papa's eyes moved down the page. Shaking his head, he had exploded.

I don't believe it!

The immigration officers had lost all his papers,

including their own records of The Interview. The letter informed Papa that he must apply all over again. Mr Nathan had been furious as well. But there was nothing Mr Nathan or Papa could do except submit a new form. Another year on, with Femi now at Avon High, Papa was still waiting to be called to Interview Number Two.

'Hey, Femi, aren't you coming?'

Gary's question jolted him. Femi had stopped near the gate. Papa's instructions were for him and Sade to wait for each other and to walk home together. Even in broad daylight, Papa was anxious for their safety. Femi scanned the students milling by the gate. On the first two days of term, Sade had been waiting there, so it had seemed quite natural walking off together. But today she wasn't there. He didn't want to say anything about Papa's instructions. Even Gary might laugh at him being treated like an infant. He turned to see if Sade was following. She wasn't. But Flash Gordon was now walking towards the gate.

'Yeah, coming.' Femi adjusted the bag on his shoulder and turned quickly into the High Street behind his friend. He knew that Sade would wait for him, like Papa told her. She would be mad. So would Papa. Well, he would just have to handle the storm when it came.

CHAPTER 2

Lizard Eyes

Sade drummed her fingers on the gate. No sign of
Femi. She was aware of an unwelcome pair of eyes,
behind narrow black shades, roaming freely over her.
On the other side of the road, diagonally across from the
school entrance, Lizard Eyes posed his long, lean body
against the wooden fence as if he were in a designer
jeans advert. Sade suspected he had chosen his position
deliberately. On the billboard above him, a silver coupé
gleamed against a spectacular golden sunset, ready to
roar across open desert dunes. He probably fancied
himself as the owner . . . among other things. The only
difference after nine months seemed to be his hair. Tight
corn plaits with little tails that looped up above his neck.
A frilled-neck lizard! She wished she had the courage to
say it to his face. But merely the thought of being within
breathing distance of him made her feel ill.

A gang of students surrounded him, all boys except
for his sister, Marcia Richards, and her friend, Donna
Layton. Both girls were in her tutor group and – like
everyone else within hearing – Sade had picked up the
gossip. A stranger listening to Marcia's tales might have
thought that her brother had gone away to a holiday

camp for a few months. The tale that no one doubted, however, was that Lizard Eyes had become a 'baby-father' while he was away. The 'babymother' had also been in Year Eleven at Avon High. But as soon as it was known that the girl was pregnant, she had dis-appeared. People said that she had gone to live with relatives out of London. Shortly afterwards Lizard Eyes also vanished. The first rumour was that he had been charged for making an under-age girl pregnant. Marcia shut up anyone who asked her but she didn't actually deny it. When the real reason for her brother's absence was printed in the local paper, however, no one was surprised. There were not many ways that a sixteen-year-old in this part of South London could afford new designer outfits almost every week.

With her back turned to the gang across the road, Sade kept her eyes trained on the glass entrance doors. She willed Femi to appear. Would he really just ignore Papa's lecture? If he had gone home ahead of her, he wouldn't be able to get into the flat until she arrived. Heaven knows who would be hanging around the stairwell. Femi had been begging Papa for weeks to give him his own key, but their father had stubbornly resisted. He wanted Femi to come home with Sade.

By four o'clock, she had started to panic. Hurrying home, she risked the shortcut between the derelict petrol station and the half-finished houses from which thieves kept stealing the building materials. Young men sometimes hung aimlessly around the old garage – one reason for normally avoiding this path, even though it saved at least ten minutes. Fortunately, no one was there today. As she came out from a stretch of overgrown grass, she could see their grey concrete block of flats, but there was no sign of Femi anywhere along the second-floor balcony. He wouldn't be waiting by the stairs because of the smell. She scanned the tarmac around the block. Children sometimes played with bikes there, but today it was empty. She breathed rapidly as she took the stairs two at a time. No one was here either. Only debris in the corners.

She was fiddling with her key in the lock, wondering what to do next, when their neighbour, Mrs Beattie, poked her head out from next door. Her pink scalp shone through fine silvery strands of hair.

'Ah, there you are, at last! I saw that brother of yours sitting outside on your doorstep. The poor mite looked quite deserted!'

Femi appeared from behind her. He avoided Sade's gaze while Mrs Beattie continued.

'I said to myself, was it not my Christian duty to ask him in? You know what types hang around here. But he's been safe with me and I've given him a good cup of tea and a biscuit.'

'Thank you, Mrs Beattie,' Femi said politely.

Sade had difficulty restraining herself until they were inside their flat.

'Why didn't you wait for me?' she demanded in a fierce whisper. The walls were thin and she didn't want Mrs Beattie hearing her shout.

Femi ambled towards his bedroom, head bent, shutting her out.

'I didn't see you,' he mumbled. 'Too many people . . . Papa is crazy!'

Before Sade could reply, he had slammed the bedroom door.

17

5 p.m.

I want to scream, Iyawo! Your eyes gazing downwards, so silently, over your polished ebony cheeks usually calm me. When I was little, I used to tell Mama that you kept watch over me. Out of all the ornaments in our home, you and your handsome bridegroom Oko were always my favourites. I sat you on my desk in my bedroom and pretended that you kept all my secrets. Mama played along with me. She said that the spirit of your forest was still alive inside you. That was why I was so happy when Papa brought you to me, all that way. Even here in London, when my fingers brush across your carved braids, I have let myself pretend that if you could just look up, your eyes would be as deep and comforting as Mama's.

But that little trick is no use today. You are just a wooden head when I need you to be flesh and blood and to have real arms to hug me! Yet, here I am, sitting opposite you, still scribbling in my book . . . 'our' book. When our counsellor Mimi got me to write my first Iyawo Book, I have to admit that you were a lifesaver. Even now, if I don't let my frustration out in writing, I am not sure what I would do. At the very least, I would burn our dinner!

Well, this evening, I don't know whom to scream at more, Femi or that Lizard Eyes! Yes, HE is back. I was hoping he would disappear forever. Stupid me. Where would someone like him go? The teachers can't do anything to him now as long as he stays outside school and doesn't break the law in front of them. (Would they even see???) He showed up right opposite the school gate, with all his friends milling round, like he is famous.

I was trapped because I had to wait for Femi. If Papa hadn't given me the Big Sister lecture, I would have just walked off. But I waited for a whole twenty minutes with Lizard Eyes leering at me. My stomach was churning all the time. I tell you, Iyawo, right then I needed to be solid ebony like you! In the end I rushed home, worrying about Femi this, Femi that. Meanwhile, he was having tea with Mrs Beattie! As soon as I asked him to explain himself, he went into his shell like a miserable tortoise with a lost tongue. Most of the time, I don't know what goes on in his head. All I know is that my happy-go-lucky, football-mad, funny little brother was left behind in Lagos and that I haven't seen him since. If the counsellor couldn't get anywhere with him, what does Papa expect me to do?

CHAPTER 3

'It's not just these local thugs I have to think of . . .'

Sade was dancing in their tiny kitchen, listening to her Walkman and waiting for the rice to boil, when Papa arrived. On weekdays, he only had an hour to rest between his day-work at the Refugee Centre and night-work driving cabs. Sade had once asked how his head didn't burst from listening to so many sad stories at the Centre.

'An information officer needs a head like a good oven,' he said. 'It gets very hot. You have to let the stories cook inside without the oven exploding.'

His image had made her smile. Papa had become a good cook in England. At weekends, he took charge of the kitchen, usually making a big pot of stew and black-eye beans on Sunday that lasted them for a few days. Sometimes he boiled yams, fried plantains or made egusi soup. He had learnt to cook as a student, but Mama had always presided over the kitchen at home. Papa tried getting Femi to help. But Femi's interest never lasted long and he would rather slip away to watch television. Later, if he complained that Papa had used too many red peppers, Papa would say that Femi should have stayed to check him. Femi's standard retort was, 'You wouldn't have listened to me anyway.' During the week, however, Sade prepared supper. Trying to involve Femi usually meant an argument. It was easier to leave him alone. Only patient Mama had known how to charm him.

The three of them sat at the small table in the kitchen to eat. Sade imagined that suppertime reminded Papa of his newspaper office in Lagos. She and Femi were the cub reporters with Papa in the editor's chair between them. He never accepted that 'nothing happened'. Even Femi knew this. Today he told Papa there had been accident in school and a teacher's finger had been nearly cut off.

'Who said it was an accident?' Sade interrupted. 'Fla– I mean Mr Gordon said there was an incident, not an accident. Weren't you listening in assembly?'

Femi gave her one of his blank looks.

'I don't have any more news,' he said to Papa.

'Did you two walk home together?'

It was the question Sade had been waiting for. She stared at Femi. Let him give Papa his excuses before she swung in! But Femi remained silent as a stone. Papa looked from one to the other, his eyes glinting behind his spectacles.

'You disappoint me,' he said quietly.

His words cut Sade. She was ready to deny, to

accuse. But her complaints suddenly boiled dry. What was the point? Papa had heard the soundtrack before. The only thing he hadn't done yet was to beat Femi.

'Bad things can happen anywhere, Papa,' Sade heard herself say as Papa's grey tufted eyebrows rose like untidy flags. 'Bad things can happen even at the school gate. We meant to walk together – but sometimes things go wrong. Like today – I was late because my English teacher was talking to me about writing a play. You should let Femi have a key, Papa! He was waiting outside the flat alone and Mrs Beattie took him in. She said it was her "Christian duty". It was so embarrassing!' Sade knew that Mrs Beattie's holier-than-thou words would irritate her father. She waited for the storm.

But it didn't come as she expected. Instead, peering at her over the straight gold rims of his glasses, he said softly, 'You know it's not just these local thugs that I have to think of . . .' His voice trailed. He didn't need to say any more. Sade fell silent. The gunmen who murdered Mama in their driveway in Lagos had long arms. How could she ever forget the voice over the phone?

If we get the family first, what does it matter?

She knew that Papa, who had always been so open in speaking out, now wrote his articles about Nigeria under a made-up name. She knew why Uncle Dele had taken a job in an art college outside London. Papa's younger brother had been in England longer than any of them. He had been active in the 'Nigerians for Democracy' movement until he began to receive death threats around the same time that the gunmen had come for Papa in Lagos. He had left London a year

21

ago and said openly that he felt safer in his small village in Devon where he was the only Nigerian. He joked how General Abacha's agents could be spotted a mile away in the countryside. But it wasn't really funny. It was because of Abacha and his soldiers that they were stuck in this small flat with windows into which the sun hardly ever shone. Why else would they want to live thousands of miles away from their real home with its spacious, airy rooms, surrounded outside by flowers with colours of sunrise to sunset? Sade no longer even asked Papa when he thought they might return. Recently they had watched a wild-life programme in which a hyena sank its teeth into the buttocks of a giraffe. Papa had said it was just like General Abacha.

That hyena won't stop until he has torn off the flesh all the way up the neck. Abacha wants to lick out Nigeria's eyeballs so there won't be anyone left to see his crimes.

Even though she had been free of her own nightmares for the past few months, Sade knew that the nightmare in their country wasn't over. Their father was not making things up.

Papa broke the silence, pushing his chair back and forcing himself up. He glanced at his watch. He was late. He would come home after midnight. No wonder his black hair had become peppered with grey in the last two years.

'Make sure you do your homework, young man, and not with the television on,' he said to Femi. 'Remember that I'm the one asking your sister to check on you – for your own good.'

Femi offered to help Sade do the drying up. He didn't even argue about going to bed. She took it as his way of thanking her for asking Papa to give him his own key. He must have been really surprised. Indeed she had surprised herself.

Friday 5th September

10.20 p.m.

Ten minutes ago Femi pranced into my room to give me a message. He is clueless!

Femi: Are you still awake?
Me: You're meant to be in bed.
Femi: A boy at school told me to give you a message.
Me: What?
Femi: He said Errol likes you.
Me (horrified): Errol who? Who told you this?
Femi: Just an older boy. I don't know his name.
Me: How did he know you then?
Femi: He asked if you were my sister. Said we looked alike.
Me: Cheek!

I flung my Bugs Bunny at him — the one with the Cupid heart that Mariam gave me for my fourteenth birthday — but missed.

Me: If he knows me, why didn't he give me the message then?
Femi (giggling): Don't ask me!
Me: What's funny? The only Errol I know of is Errol Richards, and he's no joke. His sister Marcia is in my tutor group. They expelled him last year for dealing, but he's still got friends in school. That's how he operates.

Femi avoided looking at me by staring at Bugs Bunny lying helpless on my carpet.

23

Me: Did you hear what I said? You're not telling me everything, are you?

Femi: I'm going to bed now.

Me: If it's Errol Richards, you better stay a million miles away, Femi Solaja. He's trouble. If you get into trouble, the immigration people won't let us stay!

Femi: Don't lecture me, Sade! I thought you'd be pleased.

He banged my door.

I don't like this, Iyawo. What game is Lizard Eyes playing now?

CHAPTER 4

A Present

The first thing Femi saw on the kitchen table on Monday morning was a key. It was placed in front of the chair where he usually sat. Papa's head was bent towards the little radio. Femi's first instinct was to run and hug Papa, but a tight little string inside himself held him back. He knew that Papa was going to talk to him when he had finished listening to the news. It was something about Africa. That meant Papa would be listening even more intently.

Nigerian Alpha jets attacked a ship docked in the Sierra Leone port of Freetown yesterday. A Nigerian commander claimed that it was carrying nerve gas, arms and ammunition to supporters of the military coup that forced President Kabbah of Sierra Leone to flee Freetown in May earlier this year.

Femi's ears pricked up at the mention of Nigerian jets. Normally he would not have bothered to listen.

Leaders of twelve West African states recently voted to impose a blockade on Sierra Leone. They have called for the coup leader, Major Johnny Paul Koroma, to hand back power to President Kabbah and his democratically elected government.

Nigerian troops are leading the joint West African force and have warned all ships to steer clear of Freetown harbour. Only those with food and humanitarian aid are being permitted to enter. A spokesman for Major Koroma accused the Nigerians of causing chaos in Freetown and killing civilians in the bombing.

Last week Major Koroma sent a message of sympathy to Britain on the death of Princess Diana. He said that the people of Sierra Leone would remember the Princess for her compassion as well as for her stance against land mines.

'Ehn! Ehn! Rogues and more rogues! Wolves who dress up as sheep are everywhere!'

Papa turned the volume down on the little radio. He picked up the key and held it out to Femi.

'I'm not happy about this but your sister made the case. Following in her Judge Uncle's footsteps at home! She argues just like your Uncle Tunde.' That was high praise from Papa. 'So, young man, this is your first key. Make sure you don't lose it.'

'I won't, Papa.' Femi wanted to leap and dance around but he kept his head lowered as he stretched out his hand.

'This doesn't mean that you can come and go as you please. I still want you and Sade to walk home together. This is only for emergencies, do you understand?'

Femi grasped the key and promised.

In school he showed it proudly to Gary. Gary was an only child and was used to having his own key. When he congratulated Femi, however, there was no hint of mockery. Femi felt unusually happy. With his key in his pocket, walking home with his sister no longer seemed such a burden. It was strange how he even felt sharper in lessons over the following days. The jigsaw of so many different teachers, books, rules, classrooms and corridors was beginning to slip into place. He was going to prove to his sports teacher, Mr Hendy, that he was a candidate for Avon's lower school football team. The team practised after school and Papa would then have to agree to him coming home later on his own.

He even began to think that he had worried un-necessarily about the camera-eyes' boy. He had seen him several times in the playground and learned his name when a girl had shouted, 'See you tonight, James!' She and her friends had screamed with laughter as if it were a great joke. Each time James was in a crowd and didn't seem to notice Femi. That was a relief. He was bound to ask what Sade thought of Errol's message. It would be too embarrassing to repeat what she had said, even if James's friend wasn't the same Errol. Another reason for Femi feeling easier was that the rumours about the severed finger had died almost as quickly as they had spread. In assembly Flash Gordon briefly mentioned that the police were making inquiries and anyone with information should come to his office. But it was only a sentence before a tirade on the state of the boys' toilets.

'Hey, Femi bwoy! Where've you been hiding, little brother?' James slapped his palm against Femi's hand.

'I haven't!' Femi's voice rose in denial.

'I reckoned you were bunking or something! Didn't see you around.'

James manoeuvred Femi a short distance along the corridor away from the cloakroom door that Femi had been about to enter. Femi smiled weakly. There was no escape.

'So what did she say then?' James didn't even say Sade's name. Femi felt the webbing around James's pupils close in on him. He mustn't panic. There was no hullabaloo and clamour like when they met the first time.

'Nothing.'

'Nah, come on, man, she must have said something!'

'She doesn't talk about that stuff with me.'

The older boy sucked his tongue against his teeth and shook his head in mock despair.

'If girls don't say things, you got to watch what they do! What did she do when you told her?'

'She threw her Bugs Bunny at me,' Femi said sheepishly.

'Yeeess!' James aimed a friendly punch at Femi. 'She liked the message then!'

Femi's forehead creased with doubt.

27

'You got a sister and you know nothing about girls, man! What music does she like then?'

Femi hesitated. It wasn't a question he had been asked before.

'I don't know.' He shrugged. 'Different sorts. Like girl bands.'

'You say no, no, no, no . . .' James mimicked. 'I know that girl stuff! Does she go out much?'

'Our dad is too strict.' Femi shook his head.

'Tell me about it, man!' James laughed. 'Mine was too! When he was around.' The last words had a bitter edge. Then his voice bounced back. 'Your dad's Nigerian, yeah? My friend says Nigerian dads are the worst for strictness!'

'If we want to go out, our dad must know everything.'

James nodded sympathetically. Femi took the cue.

'I want to see Arsenal play but he won't let me go with my friend. He always says he'll take me, but he's always working. Even if I want to buy some Arsenal stuff, my dad wants to check it out and then he says it's too expensive.'

'That's my team too, man!' James beamed. 'Here!' He grabbed Femi's hand and pushed something into it. 'Get some Arsenal stuff, little brother. A present, right! I'll see you around.'

Femi uncurled his fingers and stared at a twenty-pound note. By the time he looked up, James had disappeared.

Inside the toilet, Femi folded up the note tightly and pushed it to the bottom of an inside pocket of his rucksack. He would tell no one, not even Gary. Only

Uncle Dele gave him money as casually as that and never as much as twenty pounds. James must be rich! But why had he been so generous? The fuss over the teacher's finger had died down. How could taking a message to Sade be worth so much? James didn't have to give him anything. Femi felt a twinge of guilt now for complaining about Papa, especially about money. It wasn't Papa's fault that they didn't have enough here. That was why he did two jobs. Maybe it would have been better not to take James's money. But it happened so quickly and, if he tried to give it back now, James might be offended. It was all so complicated. He should try to stay out of James's way in future. In the meantime, he needed to make sure that Papa didn't find out or there would be awkward questions.

CHAPTER 5

A Little Business

The following week, instead of wandering around at break times, Femi and Gary joined a gang of boys playing football. The others were all Year Sevens and a few Year Eights, who shouted things like 'Hendy will have you for breakfast if you do that!' and 'Hendy's going to mince you up, man!' They put on a Scottish accent, mimicking the sports teacher. Some Year Eights also joked about the teacher's outdated 'Afro'. From what Femi had already seen of Mr Hendy, they weren't likely to joke anywhere within his hearing.

After their Tuesday session with Mr Hendy, Femi stood sweating beside Gary.

'All you lads could be good players if you're prepared to put in the effort.'

The teacher's black curly hair swept back from his pale brown forehead like the mane of a lion. He stood with his hands on his stocky hips, surveying the small group of boys he had called aside.

'Yes, sir!'

'Right, sir!'

'What does that mean? A, you heard me? B, you agree with me? C, you're prepared to do the work? A and B don't count in my book. All I'm interested in is C. Think about it, and if C is your answer, come to football practice on Thursday after school. You can tell your parents you'll be finished by five o'clock.'

'Well done, my boy!' Femi let Papa hug him. 'I should have practised more with you myself but –'

'It's OK, Papa.' He knew the old apology.

If only there was more time in every day!

Two pairs of red-and-black goalkeeper's gloves hung above his bed. The larger pair had hardly been used. They had been a present from Mama ... for both of them ... bought just before she died.

However, Papa had something else on his mind.

'Soon it will be dark by five and I'm not happy with you coming home alone. Perhaps you should wait at school until I come and get you.'

'No, Papa!' Femi protested in dismay. 'You may be late!'

It was true. Whenever there was an emergency at the Centre, Papa was always late. More than once he had missed his supper, rushing in and out in order to start his cab shift on time.

'Gary will be with me, Papa. We'll walk down the High Street together. You worry too much, Papa. Gary's parents –'

'What Gary's parents do is not my concern. You are my concern.'

'You gave me a key, but you think I'm still a baby!' Femi's eyes brimmed with tears.

'I hope your mother can't see us from wherever she is. She would ask what kind of place I have brought you to –' The words sounded like a bitter mouthful. Whenever Papa spoke of Mama, Femi never knew what to say. He swept the back of his sleeve roughly across his face.

'If I say yes . . .' Papa waited until Femi was looking directly at him, 'I want you to assure me that you will come straight home.'

Once again, Femi promised.

'Your word is your bond now. If you don't keep it,' Papa weighed his words, 'there will be no more football.'

After school on Thursday, Mr Hendy put Femi into defence.

'There's something terrier-like about you, lad, that makes me think you won't be a pushover.'

Femi grinned. Gary was made a forward. With Mr Hendy's voice ringing in their ears, they darted, tackled and tumbled like sworn opponents. In the changing room afterwards, while others were joking and laughing, they changed quickly. Femi had told Gary about Papa's warning.

The sky was a deep blue as they set off down the main road past the first row of small shops. Crates of yams, plantains, pumpkins and various greens were piled up in front of a grocery store. But it was the smell of suya kebabs being barbecued in the restaurant next door that brought a sudden pang to Femi's empty stomach. Sade would be preparing their meal, but nothing she cooked was ever as good as suya.

'What was my dad fussing about? It's still light,' Femi grumbled. He kicked an empty can into Gary's pathway. Gary kicked it back.

'Did your dad make you walk home with your sister when you were in your own country?' Gary asked.

'In Nigeria our dad drove us every morning in his car and –' Femi hesitated, 'our . . . our mum picked us up in hers.' He aimed the can at a lamppost. It zinged as it hit the target and bounced across the pavement.

'You had two cars! Dead rich! You never told me!' Gary exclaimed. 'That's wicked, man! How come you live here, in this council dump, then?'

Femi felt his chest tighten. He was about to say that it was too long a story when the can suddenly shot towards his foot. It didn't come from Gary. Femi peered up as James stepped out from a doorway ahead. Just beyond him was the disused petrol station.

'Good shot there, little brother. Practice makes perfect, I see.'

James blocked the pavement in front of them.

'We've been at football. That's why we're late.' Femi felt his words rushing.

'It's still early, man! What's the problem?'

'His dad said –' Gary came to his defence.

'Yeah, yeah!' James interrupted. 'I know what his dad says. Just like my dad used to, just like all dads. What's your name?'

'Gary,' Gary said boldly.

'Well, cool it, Gary. I want my little brother to meet a friend of mine. You just carry on and I'll see he gets home on time.'

Gary waited for Femi to say something but Femi remained silent.

'OK. See you tomorrow then.' If Gary felt put down, he was not going to show it.

'Yeah, see you around, man.' Femi tried to sound normal.

'Sorry to break up your one-to-one.' James softened his tone as soon as Gary was out of hearing. 'Errol wants to meet you. Don't worry, it won't be long. You'll be on your way before your dad notices a thing.'

Femi flicked over his wrist to check his watch. He felt his muscles tensing at the mention of Errol.

'Don't you trust me then?' There was a sharp edge to the question.

'I've got to be home by half-past.'

'Not a problem. Errol only wants a quick chat. You can use the shortcut.'

The shortcut that Papa said never to use. Femi's heart was thumping as fast as if an opponent's ball had just flown over his head. He followed James past three pumps that stood like solitary sentinels in front of the deserted cabin where people used to pay for their petrol. The massive roof cut out the late afternoon light. In the dimness underneath, it was already evening.

Whoever this Errol was, what did he want with him? How could he have said no?

At the far side of the building a wooden screen jutted out from the wall. That smell! It took him straight back to Alade Market in Lagos and the young men who hung around in corners smoking. As they turned the corner, a tall thin figure emerged from a door at the back of the cabin behind the screen. His toffee-brown face was almost hidden by a peaked cap and narrow dark glasses. He was dressed all in black with a black-and-white cap and matching two-tone trainers. The place looked grimy but Errol was immaculate. He left the door slightly ajar and, although no sound came from inside, Femi sensed that they were not alone.

'So this is the little brother!' Errol laughed lightly. A gold chain around his neck glinted despite the gloom. 'I've seen you around, Femi.'

Of course! This was the same young man he had noticed lounging opposite Avon after school recently, surrounded by some of the older students. How slow he was! Once or twice he had been aware of the dark glasses focused in his direction, but he hadn't been too bothered. Young men often stood on the streets scrutinizing others from behind their shades. But this was the same Errol who had sent a message to Sade. So she was the one Errol had been checking!

'Yes.' When Femi's voice finally came out, it was so small it seemed to come from a little person floating above him.

'Well, if your sister didn't point out yours truly, I don't hold it against you, Femi.'

How was he meant to reply? Errol leant backwards but his gaze didn't shift.

'Don't embarrass him, Errol, man! Look, we haven't got long because we don't want Femi in trouble with his daddy, do we?' Femi felt that hint of mocking once again. 'I've got to see to a friend so I'll leave you two together for a minute.'

A couple of young men had appeared near the old air pump and James strolled off towards them. Femi's tongue and stomach felt like they were knotted in tight plaits.

'OK, let's do a little business. Man to man.' Errol leant forward and smiled. 'You need money, right?'

James must have told him. He couldn't deny it.

'Yes.' It was hardly more than a whisper.

'Do you work Saturdays?'

'My dad won't let me.'

'Let me see what I can do for you, Femi. If James Dalton says you're his little brother, that's good enough for me.'

'Thank you.' Femi didn't want to appear rude but he glanced anxiously in James's direction.

'I owe you one, Femi. You gave your sister my message, right?'

'Yes.' It was his small voice again.

'Your sister's different. She's a good-looking girl. Like one of them African princesses – and she's got pride, man. I like that, Femi.'

'Hmmh!' A muffled sound came from the room. Whoever was inside was listening.

Femi dug his hands into his pockets. He had no idea what to say. What was this all about? Papa would be home soon and he was risking football and everything for a conversation that left him confused. Why hadn't he insisted on staying with Gary?

'I have to go now.'

'A little brother who does what he's told. I like that too, Femi. Hey, James, he says he's got to go.'

Femi turned to find James behind him.

'You finished the business, right?' James asked.

'Yeah, safe!' Errol held out his arm to slap palms. For a fraction of a second, Femi felt his hand being crushed. The gold rings that Errol wore on three long fingers pressed against Femi's knuckles.

'James will take care of you in that Avon School. No one will mess with you, know what I mean?'

Before there was time to reply, James was ferrying him away.

'I'll see you around, Femi,' Errol called as they turned the back corner of the building. The shortcut to the estate, between the unfinished houses and the waste ground, lay ahead. Femi knew he was going to be in trouble for being late.

'I'll walk with you, little brother. Show me where you live.'

At least James's arm on his shoulder felt protective outside in the dark.

Thursday 18th September

9 p.m.

How long has Papa known her? That's what I want to know, Iyawo! This evening Papa acted TOTALLY out of character. At half-past five there was still no sign of Femi. I was preparing a new tomato sauce recipe from Sunday's paper. (I want to learn Italian so have started cooking pasta.) But instead of feeling happy that the recipe was working out, I was simmering as hot as my tomato sauce. Femi promised to come straight home after his football

36

practice, so WHERE was he? My sauce tasted brilliant but I knew it would be ruined because the mood at supper would be terrible. When Papa thunders, ALL of us get drenched. By a quarter to six, however, I was seriously worried. Something must have happened to Femi. All the old questions . . . what should I do? etc. etc. Then I heard the key in the door.

Femi (his eyes darting everywhere): Is Papa here?
Me (steaming): What's wrong with you, you little —

The key rattles again. The storm is about to break loose. But instead of Papa at the door, there is a tall, elegant lady with Papa behind her, smiling like the sun is shining.

Papa: Children, this is my colleague, Mrs Wallace.

A lady with a creamy chestnut complexion (only a little lighter than yours, Iyawo) and with long, straightened black hair stands there quietly, waiting for us to say something. But both Femi and I have been struck dumb as if by lightning.

Papa (laughing): Well I never! They've lost their tongues.

He tells his lady friend our names, takes her coat and asks her to make herself at home. Femi's rucksack is still on his back and it is OBVIOUS he has just come in. But Papa doesn't say a single cross word to him! As Femi sneaks off to his bedroom, he raises his eyebrows to me. Lucky him, he's escaped. But I am left to watch Papa fuss around his friend.

Papa: Would you like tea or juice? Sade will bring it . . . Would you like to use the bathroom? Sade will show you where it is . . . You must have supper with us. Sade will put out an extra plate . . .

It was Sade this, Sade that. What has come over Papa? I felt so embarrassed. At home, Mama was the one who looked after the guests and she always did it very subtly. The four of us had to squash around the kitchen table. When Uncle Dele visits us, he jokes that we elbow each other like street-traders. But with family, that's OK.

As soon as Papa said that the lady was a journalist from Sierra Leone, Femi blurted out that we're meant to be enemies! Papa said it wasn't as simple as that. I wasn't in the mood to follow everything he said. Except that the soldiers who seized power also attacked her newspaper and arrested the other journalists. If she returns, they'll arrest her.

The lady sat silent as a statue while Papa talked. Her eyes are like that dark one-way glass you can't see through. In the end, Mrs Wallace changed the subject by asking Femi about football. What position does he like to play? What's his favourite team? Who are the best players? etc. etc. I could see Femi warming up to her. But when she asked me about my hobbies, I said I didn't have time for them. Papa gave me a strange look, but I didn't feel in the mood to talk. The only good thing about tonight was that everyone said they liked my sauce.

CHAPTER 6

What Excuse?

'James says meet him outside the Leisure Centre tomorrow at eleven.'

Children streamed by on either side of Femi in the corridor. There was no time to find out more. The Year Eight boy with the message was swallowed up in the throng and Femi had to battle on to Maths.

Gary had kept a seat for him near the back of the classroom. There was hardly time to breathe before Ms Hassan had taken the register and launched into checking the sums she had given them for homework. A group of girls near the front kept flinging up their hands. Femi let the numbers spiral across the board and Ms Hassan's words washed over him . . .

What excuse could he give Papa for Saturday? The Leisure Centre was close to the shopping mall. He could walk there in twenty minutes from their estate so he wouldn't need bus fare. But, even so, Papa insisted on knowing whatever he was doing. Papa's worrying had started almost as soon as he had come out of his prison. In those early days together, after their reunion, Femi bitterly regretted having told Papa the truth about his first few weeks at Greenslades Primary.

He had thought Papa would be proud of how he had defended himself against three bully boys and their sly taunts about refugees. At first he had ignored them. But it was when they tricked him into the boiler room that they got more than they bargained for. They thought they had cornered him. But then he had glimpsed a brush with a short wooden handle. Grabbing it, his anger had burst out. The brush flailed like a machete. His attack was so unexpected that he managed to slip like greased lightning through the astonished bullies. He banged the door and, to his huge relief, it had an automatic lock! His tormentors were locked inside! Scampering up the stairs, he had heard their shouts and hammering. He reckoned the caretaker would soon hear them. Let them explain how they came to be there!

If they laid the blame on him, he would tell everything. But the head teacher never called him. She disapproved of bullying, and perhaps the bullies were worried that, if the truth came out, they would end up in more trouble. In fact, he had no further bother with those boys again. That was why he had wanted to share his victory with Papa. Instead, by telling the tale, he had simply encouraged Papa's worries.

It had been the same in Year Six. He had begged to go to a football club on Saturdays. It was two bus rides away and Papa wouldn't let him go. It wasn't about not affording the bus fare. It was about 'trouble'. Femi had protested that he would be perfectly safe. He would mind his own business at the bus stop and on the bus. He would be fine. It wasn't fair of Papa. But Papa had an answer for everything.

Was it fair when those racist boys killed Stephen Lawrence? He was also minding his own business.

Shortly afterwards, Papa wrote an article for the *African Echo* and left a copy on Femi's bed. The headline had glared up from his pillow. 'WHAT MUST PARENTS DO?' Femi had stuffed the newspaper into a drawer. He had heard Papa's excuses. Why read them all over again? Papa said that the decision was for his 'own good'. It was the same when he and Sade were smuggled out of Nigeria. He hadn't wanted to leave, but Papa and Uncle Tunde had insisted that London would be safer. Grown-ups said what suited them. Papa just didn't want to believe that he could look after himself.

When Papa asked if Femi had read his article, he had brushed the question aside with 'No time yet'. Papa quietly asked for the newspaper back. The disappointment in his voice was unsettling. Trying to smooth the crumpled paper before he returned it, Femi had let himself glance over Papa's words.

When I was a schoolboy, I grew up believing the streets of London were paved with gold. Our teachers from England impressed on us that everything was perfect in the 'mother country'. If we were caught fighting, our teachers lectured us that 'children in England don't behave like savages'. Then they beat us!

The rest of Papa's article was about what London really was like. One sentence especially had stuck in Femi's mind.

As for savagery, when young people fight here nowadays, it is normal to use knives, broken bottles, even guns.

At Greenslades, a boy in Year Six had shown off a knife at playtime that he had sneaked out of his older brother's room. The blade was razor sharp. The boy boasted of seeing blood on it. He claimed his brother had used it to defend himself. Someone must have reported him because he was called to the head teacher's office and suspended. In Lagos, Femi and his friends had spent their time talking about football. Here, in London, boys chatted just as much about fights, gangs and older brothers. Papa might be right about the violence but, all the same, his idea of keeping his children locked up was mad. Femi had been hoping that, when he transferred to secondary school, Papa's attitude would change. Instead, it was becoming even more embarrassing. Here was James offering to take him under his wing. He should count himself lucky! No one messed with you if you had an older brother to take care of you.

Of Errol, Femi was less sure. It wasn't what Sade had said. She was just trying to be like Papa, warning him about everyone and everything. Girls were also strange. Sometimes they pretended not to like someone when really they did . . .

'Well? What answer did you get?'

Femi jerked upright. Ms Hassan's eyebrows loomed ominously close as she glanced down at his blank page. He waited, in silence, to be skewered.

'You use invisible ink, do you, Femi?'

Laughter rippled around him. Femi's fist pressed against his thigh as he shook his head. He bowed downwards, curling into himself. But Ms Hassan hadn't finished.

'You can come and show us how to work out this sum on the board. At least my chalk isn't invisible.'

There were a few more giggles. People always played with you when they thought you were weak. If he were in the same gang as James, no one would laugh at him, would they? Shuffling out of the desk, he resolved to find a way of getting out of the flat without making Papa suspicious.

Saturday 20th September

11 a.m.

> Outside my bedroom window
> flaming forest trees blaze red
> at the back of our compound.

Mama lifts one hand
to keep out the sun.
Sometimes she shakes the lemon tree.
It is a battle of wills
lemons versus Mama's long stick.
Yellow orbs tumble!
Mama catches my eye and laughs.
Outside my bedroom window now
all I see is concrete.
Even the grass is grey.

Yes, that's miserable me today, Iyawo! I thought that writing this poem would help chase my blues away but I've had to stop tears plopping on to the page. It's such a dull drizzly Saturday. Is that why I feel so homesick? And what's the point when the home you are sick for can never come back again?

Both Papa and Femi were quite cheerful this morning and that made me feel worse. Papa even agreed to Femi going swimming without any argument. Femi said his sports teacher wants them to develop as many different skills as possible. So Papa is happy that Femi is showing enthusiasm for something at last. He wanted me to go swimming with Femi but I've got masses of homework. (Every teacher is already going on about all the things we have to do just for their own subject and I've no idea how I shall manage all my course work.) Papa said he had work to do at the Centre. When I casually asked him if Mrs Wallace would be there, he looked at me curiously and then said he didn't know but 'she might be'. I suspect this has something to do with his good mood.

Well, enough diversion. I had better just get on with writing up our Science experiment. It's about water condensation. Fits me perfectly in my own damp, soggy mood.

CHAPTER 7

Stay Cool

T he assistant's eyes fastened on to Femi as he wandered over to the tracksuits. His fingers rifled through the rack.

'Can I help you? Do you know what you want?'

It was the pertness of her second question that made him prickly. She didn't appear to be much older than Sade.

'I'm just looking,' he said, staring back.

Why was she suspicious? Was it the bag on his back? Did she really think his arms were rubbery and long enough to whisk something secretly into it? He would need to be a magician. Offended, Femi took his time examining a wall of trainers, aware that every movement he made was being tracked. Finally, with his hands firmly in his pockets, he strolled out of the sports shop as casually as possible. He would not spend his twenty pounds in this shop if he could help it.

It was nearly eleven when he reached the Leisure Centre and placed himself by the entrance. Although the precinct was busy, there was no sign of James. A number of passers-by appeared to be glancing in his direction until he realized their eyes were travelling behind him to a poster.

MEGA JAM – LIVE AND DIRECT FROM JAMAICA!

A man with an African printed headscarf and oval dark glasses, another with dreadlocks and a third with a wide-brimmed black hat and white suit looked out dreamily. Femi smiled at two of their names. *General Degree . . . Cocoa Tea!* Tickets were £17.50. If he wanted to buy one, he would have enough! Not that Papa would let him go out at night.

He shifted to one side of the poster. It would have been better to meet inside the building. He would feel less exposed. What if Sade had changed her mind about staying at home and decided to come down to the shopping centre? He had said that he was going swimming and promised to return straight afterwards. He hadn't mentioned waiting for someone. He pulled the hood of his jacket over his forehead. Papa usually joked that the hood made him look like a tortoise retreating from the world. Femi knew he wouldn't joke if he could see him now. He blanked Papa from his mind. But he still felt quite visible. It needed to be winter when he would have a scarf wrapped around his neck as well. Then he could feel like he was deep inside a telescope, able to peer out, unobserved.

By a quarter past eleven, there was still no sign of James. What if the boy had made up the message or if James was just fooling with him? As the minutes now ticked by, doubt crept in. Had he been set up? Someone might even be watching him and laughing. Perhaps James was teasing him and he would have to show that he could take a joke.

By twenty-five past, Femi began to wonder whether he should leave. He could go inside and swim. Papa had given him his entrance money. If someone had tried to make a fool of him, at least he could enjoy having gone to the pool.

A burst of laughter swirled across the precinct. A posse of boys was approaching the Leisure Centre with James in the middle, wearing a smart light-grey tracksuit with grey-and-white trainers. The Year Eight boy who had brought the message was the youngest among them and he spread out his shoulders to make himself a little taller. He seemed relieved to see Femi.

'How're you doing, Femi boy?' James said nothing about being late. The other older boys all remained deadpan.

'We want you to go to the record shop.' James's eyes twinkled and scrutinized him at the same time. Suddenly it hit him. James said 'we', not 'I'. There was going to be a test.

'You know Tupac, right?' James continued. Everyone knew about Tupac. The rumours about the gangster rapper shot in Suge Knight's car a year ago had been in the news again. The picture of the slumped body had stirred horrible memories for Femi. Two sharp cracks in quick succession, screeching tyres, a scarlet pool gleaming on their own driveway in Lagos . . .

'Yes,' he whispered.

'We want the CD covers.' James wheeled Femi away from the Leisure Centre entrance and the posse clustered around him. 'Any you can –'

'Get the one with his fingers up, man, and –'

'Yeah, with his big bad face and tattoos sticking out all over his muscles!'

'Get the one where he's dressed up cool in black and white –'

'You wouldn't know he's got all that outlaw stuff underneath!'

Voices pounded around him. He felt dizzy. They wanted him to steal! They must be making pirate CDs. His head throbbed. He should have known. Idiot! Papa's eyes blazed into his mind with the pained words:

If Mama could see you now . . .

'But some shop people, they watch you like a hawk!' Femi heard the whine in his voice and tried to temper it. 'Like I was in AllSports, just looking, and the lady comes checking on me, nuh!'

'No need to tense up! We're not sending you alone!' James chuckled, then outlined the plan like a coach preparing his team. Femi was to be striker and two Year Nine boys, Jarrett and Dave, his defenders.

'So you get it, Femi boy? All you've got to do is stay cool and we score.' The shutter flicking across the black pupils in the delicate brown web reminded Femi of the first time they had met. 'Simple, right?'

It wasn't. A trap door that sucked him away would be simple. He knew he couldn't pull out now. There would be consequences.

Shoppers crowding the pavements were jostled aside as the posse cut their way through to the mall. Even those who looked annoyed moved out of their way. Femi was pinned in at the centre. The knot in his stomach felt like it was tied to every vein in his body, drawing tighter and tighter. A hundred metres from the record shop, the others melted away. He was on his own. For a wild moment he thought he might walk towards the record shop and at the last moment slip away . . . just keep walking, running. But, sooner or later, he would have to face James with his posse. He would be accused of messing them around. Femi saw the sign above the plate glass. *SOLO RECORDS*. He blasted out everything from his mind except James's instructions.

CHAPTER 8

Secrets

The words that hammered through his head bent to the beat pulsing through the shop.

Take your time
Stay cool
Femi boy
Stay cool
Take your time

It didn't take long to find the right shelf and the Ts. The gangster rapper stared up at Femi. One second his eyes smouldered, the next they looked distant and cold. Femi felt strangely hot and cold himself. His head felt like it was baking, while the nerve-endings in the rest of his body felt frozen. He needed to be alone for his task, but a girl in a short white skirt and clackety platform heels was checking out the same shelf. She gradually got closer until she hovered at his side, chewing her gum and waiting for him to finish. There was no sign yet of the two boys who were meant to help him. With only a handful of customers inside the shop, the two assistants could keep their eyes on all of them. Femi moved sideways to let the girl take his place. Slowly he flipped through the Ws, keeping the corner of his eye on the Ts. What if the girl took the covers he wanted? He would be off the hook! But the girl was simply looking and drifted off to the other side of the shop. Femi shifted back. He was alone now on his side of the counter but far too exposed. He couldn't stay here forever. Surely the shop assistants would become suspicious?

A burst of voices made everyone glance towards the door. Two teenagers – one black, one white – with identical black peaked caps turned backwards down their necks, were in the middle of a conversation loud enough to vie with the music. They both spoke with strong Jamaican accents. Five minutes ago, with James, they talked like Londoners.

'You know what I did tell her, yeah?'

'Dat gal, huh! Her eardrum so waxy you gotta say everyting twice!'

'Man, it not wax. She got rock in her ear!'

'So why you waste your breath?'

The plastic clicked under Femi's fingers. Jarrett and Dave ambled towards the assistants at the till.

'You have any old-fashioned music, yeah? For my mother, yeah. It's her birthday!' Femi heard Dave, the white boy, ask. He shunted as close to the shelf as possible.

'What kind of music does she like? Country and Western? Rock? Classical?' The assistant had taken the bait.

In one quick movement, Femi sneaked two covers under his jacket. He thrust his hands into the pockets so his fingers could clasp his booty through the lining. Then, pretending to scan the Top Ten display, he waited for a customer to push open the door. A few seconds later, he slipped out.

He had to restrain himself from running towards James at the far end of the arcade. But he couldn't stop himself grinning nervously. Mission accomplished! He would have to be careful not to give anything away here in public. When James and his friends remained expressionless, however, he was surprised.

'So where are the other brethren?'

James's question brought panic. He had hurried away from the record shop as fast as he could, without turning once to see if Jarrett and Dave were behind him. What if someone in the shop had seen something and detained them?

'You didn't say to wait for them!' Femi blurted defensively. 'I got what you wanted – and you said to meet here!'

'True. But brethen always look out for brethen.'

James stung Femi into silence. James confused him. This was the first time he had ever done something like this! The others were older and more experienced and he was the one who had taken the biggest risk.

As soon as Jarrett and Dave arrived, however, everyone relaxed. A tight gathering now formed around Femi. The covers were inspected and dropped into a carrier bag. James now smiled and Femi glowed with pleasure.

'You'll learn fast. What was that sports shop where the lady hassled you?'

The edge in James's voice pulled him up sharp. He saw what was coming and, for the second time this morning, his heart sank. James was already planning another expedition for him.

'I can't go back there! She'll know me!'

'No worries, little brother.' James shrugged. 'Someone like that can't tell one black kid from another. Hey, Gul, lend him your things.'

Before Femi could say anything further, the Year Eight boy who had brought Femi the message was holding out a blue anorak and navy wool cap. Gul was small for his age and they would fit.

As he walked beside James towards AllSports in Gul's clothes, Femi's brain seized up. The thought of what might happen if his father or sister were to see him was too much. For the moment, he was simply someone else. Under the protection of James Dalton, this 'someone else' was going into AllSports with instructions to choose something he liked for himself. James had offered to show him personally the skill in diverting the attention of a sales assistant.

The pert young woman was busy with a customer. She glanced at them but didn't look twice at Femi. An older man with a slight stoop approached them. He looked as if he would rather be sitting by his fireside at home in an armchair but he smiled and asked if he could help. James was as good as his word. He too had become someone else: a polite, well-spoken young man whose parents had asked him to take his younger brother around some shops to look for what he wanted for his birthday. It was the second birthday story Femi had heard that day. Surely this man would be suspicious? But, once again, it worked. While James kept the salesman busy with a discussion about rackets for tennis and squash, Femi scoured the shelves, searching for something that he could tuck under Gul's jacket. The tracksuits were of course too big, and so was a fine leather football. It was a toss-up between a red peaked cap and a red T-shirt. Arsenal colours. Bending down behind a rack of clothes, he swiftly stowed away the T-shirt. With his arms folded against the jacket, he sidled up to James.

'Have you found something for Mum and Dad to get you then?' James asked in his 'I'm being nice to my younger brother' voice.

'Mmmhh!' Femi nodded. He didn't trust himself to speak like James.

'Do you want to show me?'

Femi shook his head with a quick smile. Why didn't James just get out of here as soon as possible?

'Aahh! Likes secrets, does he?' The salesman put his finger to his lips. 'I used to like secrets when I was a boy.'

'Probably just wants to get back to his lunch!' James put his arm on Femi's shoulder. 'We'd better be getting home. Thanks for your advice on rackets.'

'Like I said! Piece of cake!' Back on the pavement, James was back to his usual voice.

'Where did you learn to speak like that? If that

man heard me talk, he would know you weren't my brother!' Femi's tone wavered between admiration and complaint.

'Nah! I knew you'd act the part. So what did you get then?'

Femi was relieved to find that both Sade and Papa were out when he returned to the flat. He expected Papa to question him about swimming. He would prefer to keep silent rather than make up a story. But if he didn't tell Papa something, he might become suspicious. On the other hand, if Papa found out that he was telling lies, he would be in big trouble.

Femi pulled out the T-shirt from his rucksack and laid it on his bed. If only his school football kit was this colour! He could imagine that he was playing for Arsenal instead of Avon! He would get into the team and Papa would come to watch him streaking down the field with the ball . . .

A sudden question sent his mind tumbling. How could he wear a brand new T-shirt without Papa or Sade asking him where he got it? If he had taken the cap, he could probably have said a friend lent it to him. What use was a T-shirt that he couldn't wear? How stupid! Hurriedly he rolled the shirt up as small as possible, then opened each of his drawers in turn to find the best hiding place. In the end, he stuffed it into the bottom drawer. But he banged it shut with so much force that the small photograph on top of the chest toppled over in its wooden frame. Setting it up again, he barely glanced at the figures in front of the flaming forest trees that had served as goalposts in their back yard in Lagos. Papa was standing behind Sade with his hands on her shoulders while he stood in front of Mama, cradling his football. Mama's arms encircled him. Their arms seemed to entwine.

Had Femi stopped to gaze a little longer, he might have heard Mama's soft voice.

What kind of game are you playing now? What are its rules?

Instead, he pulled the bedroom door shut behind him, made himself a peanut butter sandwich and sat down to munch it in front of the television. When Papa came home, he would tell him how Arsenal had scored.

Sunday 21st September

9.30 p.m.

Heard a horrible story today, Iyawo. We visited Aunt Gracie and Uncle Roy this afternoon and little Bonzo didn't greet us with his crazy barking and rattling the fence. Their neighbours got him as a puppy from Animal Rescue when Aunt Gracie and Uncle Roy were taking care of me and Femi. It was when Papa was locked up, because I remember saying there should also be a People Rescue Society.

Bonzo was such a sweet little Scottish terrier with white fluffy eyebrows and eyes like black shiny buttons. Aunt Gracie said that when she was a girl in Jamaica, their neighbours had a frightening big black Labrador who had also been called Bonzo. She used to joke that perhaps the Jamaican Bonzo had been reincarnated as Scottie Bonzo to cut him down to size.

Today the neighbours' house was very quiet. The moment Femi asked about Bonzo, I could tell something was wrong. Aunt Gracie didn't want to tell us but Uncle Roy said she should.

'We can't hide these things from the children, you know! Let them hear, Gracie!'

54

As soon as he said that, we _had_ to know. This is what Aunt Gracie told us . . .

Their neighbours' son Marco has got mixed up with a gang of crack dealers — and he's only my age. His parents sent him to private school because they thought that Avon was too rough. The first time we saw him in his special uniform, he looked so embarrassed. I remember thinking it was strange because in Lagos uniform was a BIG thing. He would have been really proud of it there!

Well, two weeks ago his parents got hints that he was involved in something bad. They pressed him and pressed him but he wouldn't say what it was. So, last weekend, they grounded him. His mum told Aunt Gracie that they had to lock him in his room to keep him at home. He was crying that he would be in trouble if they didn't let him go out.

Then, late Sunday night, someone kept ringing their bell and knocking on the front door until Marco's dad opened it. Luckily he had it on the chain. Bonzo stuck his head out of the door, barking and yapping. Marco's dad couldn't see clearly in the dark but he made out the figure of a man who said he had a message for Marco. He wanted Marco to come and get it. A car engine was running, out in the road behind him. Marco's dad tried to slam the door but Bonzo was in the way. Next thing, the man pulled out a gun and shot Bonzo dead!

Uncle Roy and Aunt Gracie were asleep but the noise woke them and Uncle Roy went to investigate. Marco's family was in a terrible state. His parents have sent Marco away now and won't say where he has gone because they are so frightened. I felt quite sick after I heard this. Femi looked shaken too. What harm did Bonzo ever do anyone?

CHAPTER 9

'No buts, little brother'

Femi's tears soaked into his pillow. What kind of person would shoot a harmless little dog like Bonzo? They had been friends ever since the little white terrier came to live next door to Aunt Gracie and Uncle Roy. Near the end of the long garden, behind the shed and the compost heap, Femi had found a loose plank in the neighbours' fence. By swinging it sideways, he could let Bonzo squeeze through. He only did this when no one else was around. He used to give Bonzo special treats and soon knew that chocolate biscuits and crisps were his favourites. Then they would rough and tumble. When it was time to go, he used to push the little dog back through the hole and secure the loose plank with a couple of bricks.

If others were there, Femi restricted their games to playing tug-of-war with sticks through the slits between the fence. The little terrier would bark frantically, running back and forth, calling his friend to come to the bottom of the garden. But Femi was not going to reveal their secret. Sometimes he would come back inside the house rather than drive Bonzo mad by ignoring his signals. Occasionally, from his bedroom window upstairs, Femi had watched how Marco acted with

Bonzo. Marco might throw a stick or a ball for Bonzo to fetch, but Femi never saw him pick the little dog up and cuddle him like he did.

When Papa had taken them to live in their own flat, Femi had begged to get a puppy of their own. But Papa had said it would be irresponsible. Apart from the space and the cost, what would happen if the immigration officers told them to leave the country? Hadn't Femi seen the adverts: 'A dog is for life'? He would have to wait.

Whenever they visited Aunt Gracie and Uncle Roy, the first thing Femi did was to run out to the back to see if his friend was there. But today there had been no barking. Unbelievably, Bonzo was dead. Not from running under a car or any kind of accident. Not from a disease. Not even from a fight. Someone had put a bullet through his head to send terror into the heart of the boy who owned him. Femi curled up more tightly and sobbed under his duvet.

*

'Hey, little brother, this time you've really been avoiding me! What's the deal, man?'

Femi froze in front of the bicycle shop on the High Street. It was true. James had sent a message to meet the gang in town but Femi had made up an excuse about being busy. Aunt Gracie's story had scared him. It wasn't that he believed that James, or even Errol, would do such a wicked thing as killing an innocent little dog. They might take a few things from shops and Errol and his friends smoked stuff. But that didn't make them like the gang who killed Bonzo. No, the problem with getting deeper into the gang was that it made things too complicated. Apart from anything else, how would he keep covering up in front of Papa? Life would be simpler if he just concentrated on getting into the football team with Gary. If he didn't make trouble and stayed out of the gang's way, they should realize that he was no longer interested.

'What's wrong, little brother? Didn't you hear me?'

Femi couldn't stare at the spokes of wheels behind the plate glass any longer. He half turned and lifted his face but couldn't bring himself to look directly into the brown webbed eyes.

'I haven't been feeling too good,' he said weakly. If only he hadn't stopped outside the bicycle shop, he would have already turned the corner into the estate. Then James wouldn't have caught him.

'That's what friends are for. To help you when you're not feeling so good. Errol has been asking for you.'

'I can't come now.' Femi shuffled as if he had to go.

'I've been covering for you, bwoy! I saw you look the other way twice last week but I didn't tell Errol. He doesn't like that kind of thing, you know.'

'But –'

'No buts, little brother. You don't turn down a brethren. Come!'

As they approached the garage, it appeared to be empty. The only noise came from the road behind them. The building remained silent as they walked towards the wooden screen. Femi felt the tight band around his chest ease a little. But as soon as James rattled open the backroom door, the smell of weed stung his nostrils even before he saw the fog. This time

Errol did not come out, and James led Femi inside. His eyes sharpened in the gloom. Errol and three young men were sitting on a medley of old chairs and wooden boxes. Some boxes stacked together in the middle served as a table with tins of beer and cards spread out on top. They must have been in the middle of a game because each had a set of cards in his hand.

Femi couldn't see Errol's eyes behind the shades but he could feel them penetrate him. Errol didn't make any light chat this time. He picked up a small square package from the floor and held it out. It was the size of a compact disc and was wrapped in gold paper.

'It's for your sister, right. I've been waiting nearly two weeks. Give it to her tonight, right?'

Femi felt the hardness of the parcel between his fingers.

'Right, Errol,' he mumbled.

'Just remember – I like people to stay in touch. You get my meaning?'

Femi did. He nodded. The young man sitting next to Errol had been leaning forward with his head down, hidden under a cap. He raised himself suddenly, examining Femi.

'Yeah, Errol is here for his friends,' he said deliberately. 'So his friends have to be here for him.'

Femi clutched Errol's parcel. Nothing was going to be simple after all.

CHAPTER 10

A Bad Taste

Sade found the parcel on her bed after supper. Papa had left for the cab office and she had gone to her room to continue her English course work. Had Papa left a surprise present for her? But gold paper wasn't really his style and her birthday was still months away. She guessed it was a CD. It certainly wouldn't be a gift from Femi. Yet he was the only person who could have put it there. What was going on? Curiosity fought her unease as she slipped her forefinger between the folds of gold paper to reveal the cover. Four black women in black! It was their first single. She should be over the moon! But the words in capital letters on the pink Post-It stuck in one corner made her flush as sharply as a slap.

IT'S YOUR DESTINY!
BE MY QUEEN!

A bitter taste surged up her throat like the rising of a bad memory. There was only one person who would have chosen to write those words and force them into her ears, ignoring her protests.

With the parcel in her hand, Sade stormed into Femi's room.

'Who gave you this?' she demanded.

Femi shrugged.

'A boy.'

'What's his name?'

Another shrug.

'Was it the same boy who gave you the message before?'

Silence.

'What's he look like? Is he tall? Or short?'

More silence.

'Is he white? Black?'

Continued silence.

Sade lost her temper.

'I know it's from Lizard Eyes!' she screamed. 'It's that Errol Richards, isn't it? Even if he didn't give it to you himself! I told you to keep away from him, Femi, didn't I? I'm going to tell Papa that you're getting mixed up in bad company!'

'I'm not!' Femi shouted back. 'You don't know anything!'

'You're going to make trouble for us. The immigration people won't give Papa his papers because of you!' Her voice was spiralling out of control. She hadn't meant to get carried away like this. She heard herself beginning to yell about Marco – and Bonzo dying because of him. Femi's eyes filled up with tears and he turned his back on her.

A waft of shame overcame Sade and she fled back to her room. It was Lizard Eyes she should be shouting at, not Femi. Trembling, she stuffed the parcel into her bin. Lizard Eyes was getting at her again. He was beginning to use her little brother! But what could she tell Papa? The past was the past, and better left alone. Nor did she want to accuse Femi unfairly. Who could say what Papa would do? If he let loose his temper and over-reacted, he might make matters worse. It wouldn't only be Femi who would be embarrassed. She would be too.

Sade sat down at her desk and spread out her books. She picked up her pen, trying to concentrate on what she had to do. But the disc, wrapped in gold paper and dumped in her bin, kept troubling her. She hadn't even let herself look properly at the cover with its picture of her favourite group. It wouldn't do any harm, would it? One voice in her head said, 'Don't be so uptight! Cheer yourself up, girl!' Another said, 'No way are you taking anything from Lizard Eyes!' With these voices arguing inside her, she wouldn't get any work done at all. Finally, she pulled out her Discman from her drawer and then let her hand slip into the bin. After removing the disc, she returned the cover to the bin, in case Femi came back. She just wanted to play the track once. Then she would be able to concentrate on her work.

Monday 29th September

10.30 p.m.

All evening I've been thinking: WHO is Lizard Eyes using as his go-betweeen?? Last time, Femi told me that it was an older boy who said we looked alike. Is it someone in my year? My class? I don't know why, but I've suddenly started thinking about James Dalton. He was an 'A' student until last year. He even came

62

to Ms Nichols' Book Club in Year Eight although he kept it a secret from his other friends. Ms Nichols used to announce, 'I want to see you after school, James Dalton.' She made it sound like he was in trouble but actually she was reminding him about Book Club! He was really good in the group. He picked up clues in books that the rest of us missed. Ms Nichols said that he would make a good detective. He also ate most of the chocolate biscuits that she brought for us! Mariam teased me that I fancied James more than the books but it wasn't like that. It was just more fun with him there. Then things changed in Year Nine. He only came to the club once, right at the beginning. Ms Nichols asked me if I knew what was going on with him. I don't know why she asked me. How would I know? Next thing, James had dropped down to 'B' set, so we hardly saw each other, except at tutor time. Once or twice I spotted him in the same crowd as Lizard Eyes. I was amazed. Why would he want to be friends with someone so crude and flashy? But mostly James hung out with his own crowd so I didn't really think that they could be that close.

Well, maybe I was wrong. I don't know if I'm any good as a detective but tomorrow I'm going to find out.

CHAPTER 11

Miss Daddy's Girl

'What makes you think James will listen to you? Shouldn't you tell your dad?' Mariam asked earnestly after Sade described her plan. They sat on a bench in the playground, waiting for the siren to call them to registration.

'I can't! He'd go mad! I don't know what he'd do. He keeps saying we should be at school in Nigeria where there is proper discipline.'

Sade didn't need to explain more. Mariam and her mother were refugees from Somalia. They too had been forced to escape the soldiers in their country. Mariam's mother had also been called for The Interview. The immigration officers had used an interpreter and checked every little detail in her mother's application for asylum. They had kept returning to how she could know for sure that her husband had died in prison. 'No respect for the dead.' Mariam had repeated her mother's words when telling Sade. Some months after The Interview they had received papers saying they could stay. However, Mariam still knew how it felt to have your real home far away and to have a parent who remembered it even more often than you did.

After registration, Sade lagged behind in the tutor room, pretending to check the contents of her bag. James seemed to be in no hurry to troop off to the first lesson of the day. He hung behind with a small group of students, smiling at Marcia, who was in full flow.

'This is Passion FM! Turn us on and we turn *you* on!' Marcia pouted her lips and flicked her sleekly straightened hair behind one ear. This week the black strands glinted with auburn. Her long fingers were covered in rings, four on one hand and three on the other. A cluster of gold bracelets jingled around her right wrist. Marcia managed to get away with more jewellery in school than anyone else.

'Break it up now! You're going to be late for your next lesson.' Their tutor, Mr Morris, had a stack of books tucked under one arm and was waiting to follow them out into the corridor. 'By Year Ten, I shouldn't be getting complaints of lateness.'

'Would you have liked to be a radio announcer rather than a teacher, sir?' Donna swept a comb through her long blonde hair. 'You've got the right voice for it!'

'Imagine how many people you could have driven to distraction, sir!' Marcia almost purred the last words. 'Not just a bunch of schoolkids!'

There was a burst of laughter as they headed for the door. James trailed at the rear and Sade slipped beside him. He grinned at her.

'Or driven them to grief!' he muttered through his teeth. She didn't smile back. Instead, she thrust a small piece of paper into his jacket pocket.

'Read it,' she said. 'I've got something for you. Be there.'

At eleven o'clock Sade hurried to the library. Some children were gathered around the computers and a few were browsing quietly through the paperback stand. The librarian was strict about noise. Sade disappeared between the shelves into the furthest corner with the science books. No one else was there. She picked up a book about tropical forests, but her eyes kept flicking across to the clock. By ten past eleven, there was still no sign of James. Her note had said:

I've got something for you. Come to the library at break on your own. I'll be by the science books. Sade.

The note would make sense only if she had guessed correctly that he was the go-between. He would then imagine that Femi had told her about him – and that she wanted to give him a message for Lizard Eyes. But what if her guess was wrong? It would look as if she was making a pass at James! She shouldn't have signed her name! Perhaps at this very moment he was showing the note to people like Marcia and Donna. They would all be laughing. They would probably be making a joke about Sade wanting to meet him in the library. It was probably the last place James would want to be seen nowadays. It was where they had always met for the Book Group.

By a quarter past eleven, Sade's stomach was churning and she was about to give up waiting when the entrance door swung open. James glanced casually around the library as he strolled towards the non-fiction section. He seemed completely at ease, without any of the swagger and aggression of Lizard Eyes. His face looked so open – almost innocent – that for a moment Sade hesitated. Then she pulled out the small package in its gold paper.

'Take this back to your friend.' She thrust it firmly into his hand. 'Tell him to stop pestering me. I don't want anything from him. Ever.'

Her gaze didn't leave his face. The confident brown eyes and the muscles around his mouth flickered for a moment, then settled back into a smile.

'Which friend?' he asked evenly. 'I've lots of friends.'

Was he playing with her, pretending he didn't know? However, he didn't look down at the parcel in his hand or ask what it was. That meant he knew, didn't it?

'Your friend Lizard Eyes.' The nickname slipped

from her brain to her tongue. 'Why don't you get yourself decent friends?' She stressed the word 'decent'.

His mouth tightened. The brown netting expanded and the black pupils at the centre became smaller. She had touched a nerve. She must be right. Before he had time to reply, she was going to have her say.

'You used to be worth a hundred times more than that Errol Richards. Now he's got you and you're starting on my little brother! Getting him to run your messages. I want you to leave my brother alone!'

'What are you talking about?' James retorted. 'Do you know what it's like out there on the street? Do you go around with your eyes shut or something?'

It was his turn now.

'Don't you know the streets are hard, man? You think you can ignore them so the streets don't see you? You're like that bird, an ostrich, yeah!' He was scornful. 'It takes ONE second for a boy to get cut up!'

The librarian was looking in their direction. In a moment she would come over and tell them to leave. Sade signalled for James to lower his voice.

'You should thank me if I show your little brother how to survive.' James folded his arms. His jaw hardened. How could she ever have thought that his face looked open?

'You're mad!' she hissed. 'I thought you were smart! If you don't leave Femi alone, I'll tell my dad about you and that friend of yours, and then you will be in trouble.'

'Huh, trouble? What you saying, girl? If that daddy of yours goes looking for trouble, he'll get it, right. Errol has plenty of friends, you know what I mean? They know how to take care of him. Your daddy might have

67

been a Somebody in your country, but here, he's a N.O.B . . . O.D.Y.' James rapped the letters.

She felt the blood rushing to her face.

'Do you want your daddy to play with fire? I won't go deeper than that. Join the real world, Miss Daddy's Girl!'

Sade was saved from replying by the siren.

CHAPTER 12

Hit and Run

The words hit Femi like a couple of stones in the middle of his temple. For a split second he was dazed. By the time he looked up, he caught only a glimpse of the faces turned back to him inside the car. White masks distorted with ugly laughter. Their filth was directed at Gary – but only because Gary was with him. Grown white men shouting at a white boy for walking home with a black boy.

Femi swore as the car disappeared down the High Street. It felt as if thousands of angry butterflies were suddenly beating their wings inside him. He glanced at Gary. If his friend was embarrassed, he didn't show it.

'Best to ignore people like that.' Gary shrugged. 'My mum says they're cowards. Like hit-and-run drivers.'

How could Gary remain so calm? How did he stop the foul words from getting under his skin? You couldn't ignore a hit-and-run driver when you were hit! Femi fell silent, as if an invisible screen had suddenly fallen between them. They were approaching the bicycle shop where they usually went their different ways – Gary down the High Street and Femi into the road leading to their estate. Femi stopped abruptly.

'Just remembered . . . I left my book for Ms Hassan's homework. She'll kill me if I don't do it! I'm going back. Better than getting one of her detentions and missing football practice, innit?'

'Why don't you get to school early tomorrow – and do it then?' Gary's forehead wrinkled in surprise.

'It's OK. See you tomorrow.'

Femi turned and belted away before there was any time for Gary to offer to accompany him.

As soon as the garage came into sight, he regretted coming. He shouldn't have let those racists unsettle him so much. One sudden urge to be with James, and here he was rushing into Errol's den. James mightn't even be here. Was he crazy? What was he going to tell Errol about Sade and how she had stormed at him? He halted on the forecourt, bending over to catch his breath. He could backtrack before he was seen. But it was too late. Errol had emerged from behind the wooden panel. From behind his dark glasses, he appeared to be looking past Femi at the road. He dare not turn around now. Errol had surely seen him and would take it as a snub. The butterflies trapped inside him began agitating their wings even more fiercely. Then Errol nodded to Femi, spun on his heels and disappeared behind the wooden screen. He would have to follow.

'Hey, little brother!'

Femi was relieved to hear James's voice as his eyes adjusted to the fog. James was sitting on a box next to a young man Femi hadn't seen before. Both of them were smoking. Errol remained standing. Femi hesitated in the doorway, feeling the tension in Errol. He was like a cheetah waiting to spring.

'What's the deal, little brother?' James drawled. 'You looking for me?'

'Y-yeah,' Femi stuttered. How did James know?

'I'm a mind reader, Femi boy!' James laughed. 'Take a seat.' Whatever was bothering Errol, James was not letting it get to him. An armchair with only one armrest was free, but Femi assumed that was Errol's seat. He sat down uneasily on a wooden box opposite James. Errol let out a string of curses. Femi would have jumped up again if James hadn't put out his hand.

'No need to vex yourself. Errol is waiting for some friends. Here, take a puff. Looks like you need something to calm your nerves, right?'

James held out the little white roll of paper. The smell prickled his nose and Femi rubbed the back of his hand quickly across his face. He had heard of people spluttering and coughing and making fools of themselves over their first smoke. He felt James's eyes on him, watching, waiting. But it wasn't a trick. James was only offering him what he had been smoking.

Femi stretched out his hand and secured the little roll-up between his forefinger and thumb. He raised it to his lips. One short, quick suck. Something was invading his mouth, throat, blocking his nasal passage. He was silently gasping, as if trapped inside a tight, narrow tunnel, desperate for fresh air. Then, just as it

70

became unbearable, it felt as if his head was pushing through into a larger cavern. He breathed out and gulped in new air. His head felt light. Another suck. Once again, that feeling of being trapped, then released into a haze. The butterflies that had been snared inside him began to flutter away.

'So, what's the story?'

James's voice seemed to come to him from a distance. He wondered whether James had repeated the question in order to reach him. James and the young man beside him were grinning. Only Errol remained unsmiling, hovering near the door, constantly looking out. But that no longer seemed to matter so much. Femi had come to look for James, and here he was.

'I was walking down the road, with my friend, right.' Femi hoped that he wasn't mumbling. He found it easier to focus on the empty armchair than on James's face. 'A load of white men shouted this racist stuff – from their old banger.'

'Where've you been, little brother? Black people get this rubbish every day!' James was challenging him but wasn't unfriendly. 'That's why we –'

'They were grown-ups!' Femi interrupted. 'They shouted at Gary – 'cause he's white and he was with me.'

'So what did your friend Gary do?'

'Nothing. Said just to ignore them.'

'Oh yeah? He would, wouldn't he?' James said a little sharply. Femi wondered what he meant. He was finding it hard to concentrate. He was about to ask James when his eyes diverted him, glimpsing something underneath the armchair. It looked like a half-opened gold-paper packet – exactly like the present that Errol had told him to give to Sade. Hadn't she thrown it into her bin at home yesterday evening? How could it have got back here? Femi blinked and leant forward to see through the haze. Or was he imagining things?

James followed his gaze.

'Your sister is a female lion, right! Her temper is hot, man!' James said jokingly and pretended to snarl.

Without warning, Errol veered around. He grabbed James by the front of his jacket. James hurriedly pushed himself back on his seat. His hands shot up, palms forward.

'No offence! No offence, Errol! It's a compliment! A lioness is like a queen, man!'

'Yeah, but I don't like the way you said it!' Errol released his grip as if dropping something he no longer wanted. He swung back to the door and strode out.

The sudden tension had roused Femi. He stared at his watch.

'I'm late!' He stood up but avoided looking at James. There was no way he could ask him now what he had meant by saying Sade was like a female lion. He just hoped that he could slip out to the back alley that led to the flats without Errol stopping him. Errol was scary enough even when he wasn't angry.

Femi did not need to worry. As he stepped from behind the wooden screen, a sunflower-yellow BMW with a black top swerved on to the forecourt. The windows had shaded glass, making it impossible to see inside. But when the back door flew open, Femi glimpsed that both front seats were occupied. Instead of his usual slow swagger, Errol swooped towards the car and propelled himself into the back. The door slammed and the car revved away into the High Street.

Femi whistled under his breath. It was the four-seater version of the silver BMW on the billboard opposite Avon High. A million times smarter than the dirty banger belonging to those racists. A car like that would make them dead jealous. If he had been waiting for friends to arrive in a car like that, he might also have been tense like Errol! As Femi sprinted home, it was an effort to clear his mind and think what excuse he would give for being late.

Wednesday 1st October

3 a.m.

I can't get back to sleep. My nightmare is back. I was hoping it had gone forever. It started like the old one but then I realized it was London, not Lagos . . .

I am packing my bag for school when I hear the gunshots. Mama screams. A car skids away. I drop my bag, spilling my books, pen and pencil onto the floor. I rush to the veranda. Femi is wooden like a statue. Papa is kneeling on the ground. Mama lies against him with one leg stretched out in front of her. A scarlet monster is growing all over her. Papa's hands try to stop it. But it has already spread down her white nurse's uniform. Suddenly I realize that this isn't the driveway of our house in Lagos. There are no palm trees outside the gate. I am standing on the balcony of our block of flats, in London, and Mama is lying on the tarmac below. I can hear a car revving and skidding — like it's driving around the block, circling us. Suddenly Femi and I are in the back of Papa's cab. Papa is chasing the gunmen's car through the estate. We follow it on to the High Street. I am screaming at Papa to be careful. Someone in dark glasses is watching us through the back window of the gunmen's car! The closer we get, the more I scream. I know it is Lizard Eyes.

That's when I woke up. I must really have screamed because I woke Femi up. He came to my room, still half asleep, to see what was wrong. I told him we had been chasing a car driven by the gunmen who killed Mama and that Lizard Eyes was with them. When I mentioned Lizard Eyes, it was like I'd pressed a pop-up button.

Femi (wide awake): Where was it?
Me: Outside here!
Femi (big frown): What kind of car?
Me: I don't know. Posh.
Femi: What colour, Sade? What colour?
Me: White.
Femi (relaxing suddenly): Don't worry. It's all right.
Me: There's nothing all right about it! It was horrible!
Femi: It's only a nightmare, Sade. I'm going back to bed.

I don't know what to do, Iyawo. When I try to imagine what Mama would say, she would want me to tell Papa my suspicions. But everything is so different here. That's why I thought maybe I could sort things out with James. He is definitely the go-between but I was a fool to think he'd ever listen to me. Mariam was right. It was a crazy idea. He just laughed in my face. I know that Papa can't keep Femi locked up AND my little brother has to learn to look after himself. But if I tell Papa, he will over-react and everything will get worse. It was only Mama who knew how to turn Femi round.

CHAPTER 13

An Invitation

James pulled Femi aside into the corner of the landing so other students could pass. Femi glimpsed Gary continuing up the stairs with the crowd.

'Errol's mum is away for the weekend, right. He's having a rave Saturday night. He wants everyone to come! You too, yeah.' James flicked his forefingers like twin gun-barrels at Femi and grinned. It was only a couple of days since Femi had witnessed Errol threaten James. A passing storm probably. But why would Errol want a kid like him to come to a party? Surprise and doubt must have been written in his eyes. James brought his right forefinger closer to Femi's face.

'E.V.E . . . R.Y.B . . . O.D.Y! You get it?'

His finger wagged with the beat.

'My dad will never let me out at night.'

'Oh yeah! I forgot about your dad!' James pointed his forefinger towards his own head and made a mock pistol blast. 'Well, you come Saturday afternoon – help Errol sort out the place, little brother. Meet at the usual time, usual place.'

James had turned away and was jogging down the stairs before Femi could reply.

'What was that about?' Gary asked when Femi joined him.

'He fancies my sister,' Femi lied.

Gary snorted.

'Does she fancy him?'

'Nuh, she's not interested. She says boys are only after one thing!' They both giggled.

After supper, as Papa reached for the door handle, ready for his evening shift, Femi pretended that he had suddenly remembered something.

'Oh, Papa – I've got football practice on Saturday – at school – after swimming.' He had heard Papa talking about an appointment he had in Docklands on Saturday afternoon. That meant there would be no risk of him dropping in to see the practice.

'You're going to get into that team one of these days!' Papa's face lit up. 'But I want you home by five at the latest.'

'Thank you, Papa. I will.' Femi said automatically. He was counting on luck. He didn't even know yet where Errol lived. But Sade was going with Papa to Docklands – and the chances were that they wouldn't be back until at least six.

'You will get into the team – or be back by five?' Sade asked bluntly.

'Both!' declared Femi. He smirked at her.

Friday 3rd October

9 p.m.

I'm excited, Iyawo. Papa is taking me tomorrow to meet a friend of Mama's. She's a journalist who has just come back from West

76

Africa. Papa says she'll have the latest 'inside' information. Her name is Hannah Greenwood and she worked in Nigeria after Mama and Papa were just married. I was only three when she left but I remember a photo in one of our albums back home of Mama with a white woman wearing a Nigerian wrap and buba. She has short red hair like a boy's and is laughing at the baby on Mama's lap. Me! I wish I could study that photo now. Oh, Iyawo, I wonder if we'll ever get to look at our albums again?

I hope she won't be embarrassed to talk about Mama. Apart from our family, she is the only person here in England who knew her! Sometimes I feel ashamed when a whole day passes and I haven't thought of Mama. When we first came here, her voice was in my head all the time. Like she was advising me, taking care of me. Our counsellor Mimi said it was my way of holding her close to me. She said Femi should let himself hear Mama's voice too. But maybe it was too painful for him. He used to look blank or turn away when I asked him if he remembered things Mama said. I was beginning to get worried that I could forget as well — until Papa brought Mrs Wallace home! He hasn't brought her again since then. Thank goodness. As long as they are just work friends, that's fine. I can't wait to meet Mama's friend. Papa says I used to call her Auntie Hannah. I'm going to ask her to tell me everything she remembers.

CHAPTER 14

One of the Brethren

The solid grey brick houses in Errol's road looked bigger than those in Aunt Gracie's and Uncle Roy's road, but some had peeling woodwork and a few had front gardens with pieces of broken furniture and other junk scattered among the shrubs. Even from the corner, the air vibrated with a heavy bass line pulsing out from a house halfway down the road. Femi felt a spring in his step, striding along with James and the gang. The morning had been successful. With Dave, Jarrett and Gul, he had collected a batch of new CD covers from two different record shops. His stomach had still been knotted but his head had been much clearer than last time. Today he had been able to predict each move. He also told himself that he didn't need to be so worried. After all, they were only taking empty plastic cases.

It was a warm day and the door to Errol's house was open, letting the music surge out. Two small boys were chasing each other between the entrance and the pavement. When they spotted James, they came tumbling up to him. He ruffled their hair and pretended to spar with both of them at the same time. They looked like twins. They danced around James, laughing as if he were their captive, not allowing him to enter the house. However, as soon as Errol appeared at the door, they pulled back and dashed away to the pavement.

Errol showed none of the tension Femi had seen earlier that week. From his shades to his shoes, once again he was dressed in black. This time there was a matching silver stripe down the side of his jacket and trousers and diagonal silver stripes on his trainers. Each time Femi had seen him, Errol was wearing different clothes. His den at the garage was shabby but he always took pride in how he looked. He wasn't wearing a cap today and the zigzag of tiny plaits reminded Femi of what Sade had called him. *Lizard Eyes.* But why did she pick on his eyes? You could hardly see them behind the slender dark glasses. Surely it was his hair that was like the amazing pattern of a lizard skin!

They followed Errol into the hallway, with the music pounding down the stairs and into the sitting room. Errol pointed to a cream leather settee and armchairs. As Femi perched next to Dave and Jarrett, his eyes sneaked around the room. It was smart. The television looked almost twice as big as the one Papa rented. A neat silver stereo system sat on fancy steel-and-wooden shelves, next to a stack of CDs. A large gold clock ticked on the mantelpiece with a row of china ornaments on either side. Everything looked as if it had been bought new – unlike the second-hand furniture that Papa had bought or been given for their flat.

Errol explained the plan. They needed to clear out all the furniture into a small porch at the back. The ornaments were to be put upstairs, in his mother's bedroom.

'My mum likes to keep the place nice. I don't want her freaking out when she comes back, right.'

'Did you tell her? Hundreds of people raving in her house, man!' James rippled his shoulders and arms.

'Yuh tink I stupid!' Errol laughed, making a mock punch at James. 'She won't know a ting, bwoy!'

Errol obviously didn't have neighbours like Mrs Beattie, thought Femi. If he ever played music loud enough for Mrs Beattie to hear, she would be sure to tell Papa when he came home. Or did Errol have so much power over his neighbours that they didn't like to make a fuss?

When Errol instructed him to move the ornaments, Femi wasn't sure whether to feel flattered or nervous.

'My mum's bedroom is straight above, right. Put them on her dressing table and don't touch anything!'

As if he would! At each end of the mantelpiece, a china cat sat upright, ears alert. One white and one ginger. Femi carefully took one in each hand. He checked each step going up the stairs. Just as he reached the top, a girl's voice startled him.

'D'you know how much those are worth? Antiques, you know. My mum will kill you if you break them!'

A girl with honey-brown skin and a face framed with silky black hair stood in the doorway of a room along the landing. She wore a very short red skirt and black patterned tights. A pale white girl with startling black eyeliner looked over her shoulder. Of course! Errol's sister and her friend in Sade's tutor group. The girls who gave his sister such a hard time when she had been new at Avon.

'I'm helping Errol,' Femi said, clutching the cats closer to his chest.

'He's Sade's little brother, ain't he, Marcia?' The friend fingered strands of vanilla-coloured hair that hung down to her shoulders. The other half of her hair was plaited. It looked as if she was in the middle of having her hair done.

'Yeah, Sade used to really fuss over him! Like she was his mother! Remember, Donna?'

'How come he's friends with your brother, then?' Donna asked.

'Errol fancies Sade.' Marcia shrugged. 'I told him he's wasting his time.'

They were talking like he wasn't there. He wanted to tell them to get lost but he didn't want a confrontation. He scanned the open doors as he reached the landing. Bathroom. A room with bunk beds and a clutter of toys across the floor. Then Marcia in her doorway. Beyond her, a room with a white satin bedspread and a dressing table with gold trimmings. Finally, a small room with music equipment stacked up the walls. He had to get past Marcia. His palms suddenly felt sweaty and the cats a little slippery. Would she block his way?

'Excuse me,' he said, walking on but not looking at her now. She let him pass but called out as he entered the next room.

'You don't know my mum's temper, boy! If she knew you had been into her bedroom –' Marcia finished her sentence with a long, ominous whistle.

Femi lowered the cats gently on to the glass-topped table, hardly daring to look around. Then he hurried back downstairs to the front room. Errol lifted the gold clock off the mantelpiece. It looked heavy.

'Have you just got one sister?' Femi asked, stretching out both hands to take the clock.

'Yeah, she's enough. Did she give you grief up there?'

'Nuh!' Femi turned for the stairs and took a deep breath. To his relief, Marcia had disappeared and her door was closed.

When the front room was empty and the carpet rolled away, Errol handed round cans of beer. He held one out to Femi. How could he say he didn't drink beer? Or, rather, that he hadn't drunk beer before . . . and that his father would be horrified? Femi took the can. He watched the others opening theirs, including Gul, who was only a year older than Femi. If he hesitated any more, someone would say something. Femi hooked his forefinger under the metal ring and pulled. He saw the froth rising and took a swig. Ugh! Bitter! Foul! It took an effort not to spit it out! Fortunately the others were chatting. No one was even looking at him, and the next thing they were all tramping upstairs to see Errol's music equipment.

Two enormous black speakers loomed over the room from each end. On the shelf between the speakers were an amplifier, a tape deck and other equipment with dials that Femi couldn't identify. On a table below were two record decks, a synthesizer and headphones. Errol put on a pair of headphones and sat down. At first Femi crowded round with the others, watching as Errol's fingers hovered, swooped and whirled over a couple of discs. He took sips from his can, getting himself used to the flavour. After a while, it no longer seemed so bad.

He was glad, however, when Gul pulled out of the group and sat on Errol's bed. Femi joined him, lying back against some cushions. He was feeling a little light-headed and the bed was reassuring. The room was small and the bass rhythm so powerful, it was like being inside a beating drum. He wanted to close his eyes to let the music seep in more deeply. But he was worried that he might fall asleep and he fought against letting his eyelids drop.

Loud thumping up the stairs and a flurry of wailing and yelling made Femi sit up. The two small boys who had been playing outside ran tumbling into Errol's room. Each accused the other of having started a fight. James stepped in between them, holding one away from the other.

'Hey, cool it, little brothers!' James laughed.

'Stop that bawling!' Errol commanded. He took off his headphones.

The little boys fell quiet for a moment, still pulling faces at each other, until one cried, 'I'm starving. Can I have something to eat please, Errol?'

'Please!' pleaded the other.

Both boys put their hands on their stomachs and changed their faces into looking pained.

'Ask Marcia to make you a sandwich then.' Errol lifted his headphones, ready to put them back on again.

'Oh yeah. Ask Marcia, she'll do it! When do *you* do anything?'

Femi's head swung towards the door. Marcia stood there with a hand on her hip, just like when she had challenged him earlier on. But this time she was tackling her big brother. In front of his friends, too. No one moved, including the little boys. Only the music kept pounding through the room until Errol swivelled his chair, turned off the music, and swivelled back to face Marcia.

'What's your problem, Marcia?' He leant back, his arms hanging over the armrests. Femi felt Errol's eyes alert and sharp behind the shades.

'I said "When do *you* do anything?"' Marcia stared back at her brother.

'Listen, girl, it's simple. I do my own thing, right. I live here and I contribute. Money, right. You don't tell me what to do! It's nothing to do with me if Mum chooses to go away and leaves you to be mummy.' He was sneering at her.

'They're your brothers too!' Marcia's voice rose. 'I thought you'd want to get some practice, Mr Baby-father.'

No one moved.

'You want me to hang out *your* dirty washing on the line? There's plenty, plenty.' Errol repeated the word, slowly, deliberately. It was a warning. 'You better mind your own business, girl, and get lost.'

'Right, I will,' Marcia said brashly. 'I'm going out tonight with Donna. You're not the only one who's got a rave. Isn't that so, Donna?' Marcia looked behind her. Femi couldn't see anyone. If Donna was there, she must be hanging back.

'So what about the kids then?' For the first time, Femi could hear from Errol's voice that he was rattled. 'What will Mum say when she hears you left them on their own?'

'What will she say when she hears you had a rave in her house?' Marcia turned and flounced off. 'Come on, Donna! Bring my jacket.' For a couple of moments the only sound was the clatter of footsteps down the stairs.

James broke the tension.

'Whoosh! Volcanic!' He put his hands together in

front of his face and pretended to blow them apart.

He took the little boys by the hand again and winked at Errol.

'I be chef! Take me to your kitchen!'

'Yeah, thanks, my bro'!' Errol grinned. If he was embarrassed, he wasn't going to show it. 'Women! Their tempers can burn you, man!' He shook his head. 'Men have got to handle everything! You get me?'

Femi laughed with everyone else. Errol swivelled back to his decks. When the music blasted out again, the bass line beat fiercer than ever.

It was half-past five when Femi remembered to look at his watch. He was already half an hour late and it would take another half-hour to get home. He still felt a little unsteady on his feet, although the cheese and ham sandwiches that James and Errol's little brothers had made for everyone seemed to have helped. When he mumbled that he had to go, he was relieved to hear Gul say he had to go too. At least he wasn't alone. However, Gul announced that he might be back later. Gul didn't seem embarrassed and it was only Femi that James teased.

'Home to Papa, little brother – and to that Little Mama sister of yours?'

Femi felt himself flush, tongue-tied. When had he let slip the word 'Papa'?

'Here, chew these!' James beamed and held out two small green oval capsules. He pretended to sniff Femi. 'Don't go breathing all over them, right!'

Two little liquid green eyes rolled in James's palm, staring up at Femi. Imagine breathing over Papa! It was so ridiculous that giggles bubbled up through

his throat. Almost gagged him. Everyone laughed, even
Errol, as Femi popped the capsules into his mouth. He
removed his other hand that propped him against the
wall. He wobbled slightly, then grinned sheepishly.

'See you, brethren!' he said, slapping palms with
James.

CHAPTER 15

Across the River

Sade was surprised at how happy she felt as she and
Papa boarded the red double-decker bus. In Lagos,
she had occasionally gone to his newspaper's office
and, more rarely, had been allowed to accompany
him when he was investigating a story. She had loved
visiting parts of the city and people she didn't know.
It had been such a long time since she and Papa had
gone on an expedition together.

Sade led Papa to the front seat at the top of the
bus. From here they had a bird's-eye view of the road
ahead and throngs of people bustling below with
Saturday morning shopping. As the bus crossed the
river at Tower Bridge, rumbling towards the Tower
with its turrets and ancient stone walls, it felt as if they
were entering another world. They climbed off at the
next stop, mingling with the tourists with cameras
slung over shoulders and an air of being on holiday. A

couple of ravens squawked overhead, flying towards the entrance of the Tower. Last summer, when Uncle Roy had brought them all on a trip here, Sade had said that the cawing made her think of the cries of people whose heads had been chopped off inside the Tower. But when the guide invited them to admire the brilliance of the diamonds in the Crown Jewels and the Royal Sceptre, Papa murmured that the ravens could be cawing for people in Africa too.

How many people have lost their lives because of diamonds? If only we could eat the wretched stones, they would offer us life, not death!

Today they left the Tower behind them, mounting the stairs to Tower Hill station. As the train raced along a track high above the ground, propped up on giant concrete stilts, outside the windows was yet another world, one still being created. Glass-and-steel, shimmering new constructions swept Sade's eyes skywards above crumbling brick buildings and yards of rusting iron below that had once been part of London's docks. Cranes peered in all directions across the landscape like gigantic stiff-necked giraffes. The docks were no longer in use, said Papa, but billions of pounds were being spent on new offices and homes.

'Femi should have come with us,' said Sade. 'He'd have liked this.'

The River Thames stretched away, glinting like beaten silver, on their right. Somewhere on the other side of the river, in the hazy distance, was their flat, Avon High School and the Leisure Centre where Femi would be swimming.

'It's much better that he's training and working hard for his sports teacher. At last, he seems to be making an

87

effort. Tell me, Sade –' Papa waited for her to shift her gaze away from the view outside. 'Is Femi beginning to settle down at Avon?'

Papa's directness caught her unprepared.

'I don't – I –' She hesitated. To talk about her fears now would spoil the atmosphere. 'Femi doesn't say much, Papa.' At least that was the truth. 'But I know he wants to get into the football team. Remember how he and Kole used to pretend they were going to play for Nigeria?'

'Well, let's hope he is turning the corner.' Papa smiled.

'How many stops after Canary Wharf, Papa?' Sade smothered a twinge of guilt and changed the subject.

They descended to ground level beneath the massive concrete pillars. The streets here seemed strangely deserted. In one direction, a line of lonely cottages clustered together as if ready for a last stand. They faced a corrugated-iron fence, behind which the bulldozers had already reduced the buildings to rubble. In the opposite direction, tall, sand-coloured apartment blocks stood freshly cut out against the blue sky.

'This way,' said Papa, pointing to the new buildings.

Papa held out his arm and Sade slipped hers through his.

'Tell me again how you and Mama met Aunt Hannah. You were still at university, weren't you? I want to ask her lots of questions about when you were young!'

'Are you practising to be a journalist?' Papa chuckled. His face was looking more relaxed. He was also enjoying their outing together.

The woman who opened the door could have stepped out of the photo that Sade remembered. Her autumn-red hair was cropped round a neat oval face and her green eyes, flecked with brown, danced with pleasure. She was wearing a black jumper and jeans, not a buba and wrap. But she didn't look much older than in the picture. Sade felt a sudden pang as she watched Papa hug her. If Mama were still alive, she would look young too.

'Sade! Almost as tall as me! How wonderful!'

Warm, strong arms enclosed Sade. When Hannah Greenwood released her, Sade saw tears misting her eyes.

'You look so like her, you know.'

Sade didn't know what to say, but she was smiling, blinking back her own tears and smiling. Then suddenly her gaze travelled past her parents' friend to the upright figure of a woman in front of large glass doors. The light was behind her so her face was in shadow. But she was unmistakable. Mrs Wallace.

CHAPTER 16

Muddy Water

'You've met my friend Cynthie Wallace, haven't you, Sade? Your daddy's colleague. Small world, isn't it?'

The two women were old journalist friends, Aunt Hannah explained, from the time when she had left Lagos for Freetown. Mrs Wallace stepped forward with an amused smile. In a tailored cream suit, she looked as stylish as when Papa had brought her to their flat. Sade tried to hide her irritation and disappointment. She had known Papa was coming to get news, so why should she be surprised if a colleague from the Refugee Centre was there as well? Especially if that person was Mrs Wallace. She had let herself be carried away by her private fantasy.

As Papa and Mrs Wallace settled down on the sofa, Aunt Hannah turned to Sade.

'Will you help me lay the table, please, Sade?' Her voice had a light, friendly lilt. 'Lunch first, work later.'

Sade avoided looking at the sofa as she followed Aunt Hannah into the kitchen.

'Do you like singing as much as your mother, Sade?' Aunt Hannah asked the question as simply as if she was asking whether Sade liked ham or cheese. She was opening a door to talk about Mama. But instead of saying 'Yes, I love singing!' and asking Aunt Hannah what she remembered Mama singing, Sade lowered her eyes and shrugged. As soon as she had made the gesture, she regretted it. It was a clear put-down, a sign that she didn't want to talk about Mama, that she found it too upsetting. Before she had time to retract, Aunt Hannah sensitively changed the subject to what they needed to put on the table.

Over lunch, the conversation revolved around 'old times'. It was mostly about the cat-and-mouse games played between the military government and journalists. Sade listened in silence as the adults shared tales of police raids, newspapers being closed down, writers publishing 'underground', fleeing or being thrown into jail.

After lunch, when the conversation turned to the war in Sierra Leone, Sade slipped through the plate-glass doors outside on to the balcony. She leant over the railings, staring at the patio far below, dotted with ornamental palm trees, then at the river and beyond, over the rooftops of south London. Occasionally a tug, a barge or a boat full of sightseers sailed past. The water had looked silver from a distance but closer up it looked muddy and dirty. Appearances were deceptive. It was like that with people too. Could people ever really understand each other? Even in the same family? After all, she didn't understand Papa or Femi, or even herself. She turned to go back inside.

Through the plate-glass door, Sade saw the three adults focused on the television screen. As she stepped into the living room, Aunt Hannah paused the video.

Horizontal lines blurred over the face of a young black boy.

'I hope you won't find this too disturbing, Sade. I was interviewing child soldiers in Sierra Leone. Would you rather go to my study?' Aunt Hannah offered. She wasn't being patronizing. Just offering an alternative.

'I'll watch,' said Sade. Her mood could hardly get worse.

Mrs Wallace edged closer to Papa to make space for Sade on the sofa.

'I prefer this.' Sade pulled up a stool near her father.

The boy on the screen emerged with a shaved head and dark, empty eyes like gun-holes. The camera didn't show Aunt Hannah but Sade recognized her voice.

'What did the rebels tell you to do?'

A young man standing next to the boy translated the question and the boy's answer. Both their voices were matter-of-fact.

'They gave me matches. They told me to put my house on fire. My father was inside. I said "No! I can't burn my father." Then one of them put a knife here.'

The boy ran his forefinger under his chin.

'I made the fire. I wanted to pull my father out of the house but they held me. My father was crying for help. Then I couldn't hear his voice any more. Only the fire eating up the house.'

'What happened to your mother?' Aunt Hannah asked gently.

'They took her – into the bush. She was screaming. They killed her.'

The boy buried his head in his hands and remained silent.

The camera moved back and showed a group of four boys with Aunt Hannah.

'Can you tell me what you did when you lived with the rebels?'

'Yes,' said a boy in a faded red T-shirt with a hole under one armpit. 'They showed us how to cut off people's arms – with a machete – like so.' He demonstrated a quick movement with his hand across his opposite arm. If they didn't obey, their own arms would have been chopped off. Each time, before an attack, the rebels made them take drugs. That way, they didn't feel so scared.

'Were there girls as well?'

The red-shirted boy nodded.

'They did cooking. Cleaning. The leaders took girls to sleep with them.'

'What happened if a girl said no?'

'They killed her.'

'What do you want to do, now you are free?'

Three boys said that they wanted to find their parents, to see if they were still alive. The boy with the gun-hole eyes said nothing until the others looked at him, waiting.

'I want to go to school,' he said.

The screen flickered and went blank. No one said a word. When Sade glanced up, she saw that Mrs Wallace's cheeks were wet. Her eyes were closed but tears were trickling down. Papa pulled out a handkerchief from his jacket pocket and pushed it into her hands. Mrs Wallace began to dab her cheeks. Her hands were trembling. Embarrassed, Sade rose from the stool.

'Those boys –' Mrs Wallace whispered, '– they look the same age as my Edward.'

Sade saw Papa's arm encircle Mrs Wallace and hold her tight. Without a word, she fled back to the balcony.

Saturday 4th October

10 p.m.

> If the sun shines when you enter the forest, don't be
> sure it will shine when you leave.
> – ONE OF MAMA'S PROVERBS

Today turned upside down. I felt so happy this morning, going with Papa to see Aunt Hannah. My head was like a hive of bees, full of questions. But then I saw that SOMEONE ELSE was there. Yes, Mrs Wallace. My questions vanished and I messed up my chance of talking about Mama. Aunt Hannah showed us her video of child soldiers and Mrs Wallace got into such a state that Papa insisted she come home with us! He kept saying, 'We can't let you go back to your lonely room while you are like this!' How did Papa know it was a 'lonely room'? Who did he mean by 'we'? I didn't say anything.

Femi was already in bed when we came home. He told us he had a headache from concentrating so hard at football. He said he had eaten a sandwich and wanted to sleep early. Papa said, 'Good boy!' and left him alone. Afterwards I bumped into Femi by the bathroom. His breath smelt funny but he skipped off like a rabbit before I got another whiff.

Papa has now spent the whole evening with Mrs Wallace. He cooked one of his stews and she helped him. I said I wasn't hungry but I could tell that Papa was going to make a fuss if I didn't eat with them. It was unfair because he let Femi off. All the time they kept talking about Sierra Leone and what articles they would write about child soldiers. Papa was getting very steamed up, like when he wrote his articles at home. But at least Mama knew how to calm him down, not stir him up even more. They were perfect together, weren't they, Iyawo? They balanced each other. If something was wrong with me or Femi and if Papa didn't notice, Mama always talked to him and then he would understand. But Mrs Wallace and Papa just keep talking about the war as if it's the only thing going on. It's almost eleven o'clock and I can still hear them. When is she going home???

CHAPTER 17

Charm

Femi unfolded and smoothed the creases out of his new T-shirt. Even without the Arsenal logo, it looked smart. If he didn't come up with a good story soon about where it had come from, he would outgrow it, and it would be wasted! A knock at his door and Sade's voice made him hurriedly stuff it back in the drawer under his bed.

'Why do you wake me up so early?' He stretched his arms, pretending to yawn, as Sade entered.

'You're up. I heard you!' She closed the door behind her.

'Are you spying on me?'

'No! Have you something to hide?'

'Go away, Sade! I didn't say you could come in!' Femi said irritably. He folded his arms, kneeling near the drawer.

'OK, OK, I'm only teasing!' Sade sat down on his bed. 'Listen, Papa has a girlfriend. He's been talking and carrying on with Mrs Wallace like he used to with Mama!'

Femi frowned.

'So what?'

Sade stared at him.

'He's beginning to forget Mama, that's what! You should have seen him yesterday – getting carried away with this war in Sierre Leone and all the bad things there. Mrs Wallace is taking advantage of him.'

Femi shrugged.

'You can't tell Papa what to do.'

'Don't you care? Don't you understand what I'm saying?' Her voice was rising.

'You're just jealous, Sade. Typical woman!' Femi grinned. 'Papa's a man. He can do what he likes, you know.'

The words were out before he had even thought about them. His sister's face wrinkled in disgust.

'I don't know where you've been picking up this sexist stuff, Femi Solaja! You think that if Papa is busy with a girlfriend, he won't see what you get up to! But I smelt your breath last night. You –'

'You smelt nothing!'

'I know what I smelt and I can tell Papa what I know.'

'Well go ahead, Miss Know-All. Leave me alone. Get out!'

As soon as Sade left the room, a cloud descended on Femi. He punched his fists into his mattress. He should have been more careful not to get into a stupid spat with his sister. James was expecting him to come to Errol's house this morning. They were going to sort it out for Errol before his mum returned. James had said that Errol would 'appreciate the gesture' if Femi came along. Last night his brain had been too fuzzy to work out what reason he could give Papa. But now, after Sade's threat to speak to Papa, anything he said would be too risky.

Femi resigned himself to a day indoors. There was nothing to do except watch television. However bored he was, he wasn't going to ask Sade if she wanted to play Ayo or anything else with him. Mrs Wallace arrived mid-morning, and she and Papa busied themselves at the computer in Papa's bedroom, working on an article. Sade's door remained closed until Femi heard Papa asking her if she would make them all some lunch.

He detected his sister's mood from the banging and rattling in the kitchen. It didn't sound good. He waited for her to tell him to set the table, but she didn't. Instead, he heard more clattering of plates and cutlery. In this mood, she could say anything to Papa. It would be wise to make up to her.

Sade put her head round the kitchen door.

'Tell Papa lunch is ready,' she said stiffly. She didn't mention Mrs Wallace.

The small kitchen table had to be pulled away from the wall to fit in the fourth chair. His sister had not pulled it out very far.

'Will you be able to squeeze in there, Sade?' Papa asked.

Sade didn't answer. She turned away to pick up

the pan with scrambled eggs as if she hadn't heard. Instead of repeating himself, Papa joked.

'Perhaps I am slim enough myself! If I don't fit, it means I need to diet!'

But before Papa could try, Femi slid into the seat.

'Good child.' Mrs Wallace gently pressed his shoulder. 'You won't let your daddy show himself up, will you?'

Only Sade didn't smile. She dished out in silence, not even responding when Mrs Wallace thanked her. Papa frowned and Femi wondered if he would say something.

'So, Femi, how is football?' Mrs Wallace turned to him, breaking the silence.

'It's good.'

'Your daddy says you will soon be in the school team! Is that so?' Her dark eyes squarely invited him to carry on. He began to talk about how he and Gary wanted to get into the team together. Then Mrs Wallace asked what else he liked at school.

'Science. Gary and I like experiments. Gary never gives up! He's mad!' Femi shook his head, smiling as if at a private joke. 'One day he nearly exploded a television set! He was trying to fix it . . .'

Femi surprised himself. Once he got started, he could go on! He was enjoying spinning out the story. He wasn't going to spoil it by saying that it had actually happened way back in primary school. Mrs Wallace seemed amused and Papa was beaming. Only Sade looked unimpressed.

'How do you find your school work here, Sade?' Mrs Wallace was obviously not one to give up easily.

'Fine.' One short, sharp word. That was all. Sade did

98

not lift her eyes from the table. An electric current seemed to pass across Papa's face. Femi held his breath. Serve Sade right if Papa told her off! Then Papa's face relaxed again.

'Femi is a first-class storyteller, isn't he, Mami Cynthie? I've always thought Sade would make a good journalist, but maybe my son will follow in my footsteps!' Papa stretched out his hand and patted Femi.

'Now, pardon us. Mami Cynthie and I don't have much time.'

For the rest of the meal, the adults talked about their article. Afterwards, when they had returned to Papa's computer, and Sade to her room, Femi settled back in front of the television. He must have a lucky angel looking after him! He had been very worried that Sade was going to tell tales. Instead he had managed to charm Mami Cynthie – and Papa! If he had made up a story about going out, Papa might have believed that too! But it wasn't worth the risk. He wondered if Errol's house was already sorted. Papa and Mami Cynthie were writing about children being captured. Sometimes he felt captured. It wasn't the same, of course. James said he should challenge Papa more. But maybe it was easier to charm him.

Mami Cynthie waved to Femi from the front door before leaving.

'Say goodbye to Sade for me, please.'

Looking up from his cards laid out on the carpet, he lifted his hand and smiled. He wasn't going to tell her that it would be a crazy thing to do. Papa followed her out of the front door. If Sade was right that she was now Papa's girlfriend, he was probably kissing her goodbye. Femi couldn't imagine it. He wondered about creeping up to the window. But if Papa saw him behind the net curtain, it would be asking for trouble.

Papa wasn't long. As soon as he came back in, Femi saw him enter Sade's room. Femi levered himself up and tiptoed down the corridor. The door wasn't completely shut.

'This is not like you, Sade. Why were you so rude to Mami Cynthie?'

There was no reply. Femi bit his thumb.

'Have you nothing to say?'

Silence again.

'I'm used to silence from your brother but not from you, Sade.'

Femi thought he heard Papa sigh.

'Mami Cynthie was too polite to say so, but I could see that you hurt her,' Papa continued in a firm, clear voice. 'She was already hurt by the interviews we saw yesterday. She doesn't tell most people but I think you should know. She has a son – about Femi's age – the same age as those boy soldiers. That's why she was so upset. Her son Edward is in boarding school in Sierra Leone. She hasn't seen him for over six months and she doesn't know when she'll see him next. Try to imagine what that feels like, if you can.'

'He's in boarding school, so at least she knows he's safe,' Sade blurted. She sounded very offhand.

Femi pinched his folded arms. His sister didn't usually talk to Papa like this.

'I am surprised at you, Sade, and deeply disappointed. I thought you were more mature.'

The handle on Sade's door wobbled and Femi scuttled into the bathroom.

Sunday 5th October

8.30 p.m.

Papa says he's disappointed in me! Just because I didn't want to talk to Mrs Wallace. They spent the whole day together in Papa's room, writing an article on child soldiers. I'm not saying they shouldn't try to stop things like that going on. But if Papa has time to investigate all these stories of children in Sierra Leone, why doesn't he investigate Femi? It was so <u>obvious</u> that Femi was putting on his charm. He even called Mrs Wallace 'Mami Cynthie'. Mama would have seen through him right away. If Papa is too wrapped up in Mrs Wallace to see anything, why should I bother?

To tell the truth, Iyawo, it's me who should be disappointed in Papa. Sunday is meant to be our family day. We don't go to church like we used to with Mama, but this is the one day that Papa has free for us to do things together. Papa doesn't know how lucky he is to have a daughter who wants to spend time with her father! Most girls my age in London don't want to be even <u>SEEN</u> with a parent. Most of them go out with their friends, raving and whatever, every weekend. Some of them are out every night. The next day they'll be talking about who they were with, how this girl went off with this boy, what they did etc. etc. (It's like the whole point is for everyone else to know.) But me, I stay at home, like Little Miss Perfect, cuddled up with my course work so I can get all those 'A' grades that my teachers and Papa expect. If I'm honest, I expect those grades from myself. I only go out with Mariam or my family. Papa always knows where I am. So, I'm still a good Nigerian daughter! I even get called 'Miss Daddy's Girl'. Papa doesn't appreciate what I go through. When I was little, I used to think he understood everything. But then he had Mama's eyes to help him.

Sometimes I think maybe I should have told him last year about that disgusting thing with Lizard Eyes. Mariam kept urging me to tell him but I didn't know how. Then Lizard Eyes got himself

101

expelled for dealing. I know people in my class say things like 'Oh, I've never seen Sade with a boyfriend' and 'Sade is frigid'. Just because I don't mess around with boys like they do. I try not to show it but it hurts and if they say it enough, you begin to doubt yourself. Anyway, I don't want to be like them. When they get older, I think the same boys will disrespect them because they were so easy and just gave them everything they wanted. Lots of boys want it both ways. They want girls for a good time but, when they want to settle in a steady relationship, they want decent girls who they know won't play around with anyone else. I never want to be anyone's plaything! But I'd still like to have someone to talk to and hug me when I'm down. I just haven't met anyone like that yet. That doesn't mean I'm no good at relationships.

You know how different it is at home, Iyawo. Over there, our family was like a branch of a giant tree. Grandma and her generation were the trunk. All our aunts, uncles and cousins filled up our branches. All our friends from school, Mama's church, her hospital, Papa's newspaper and their families filled up the other branches. Whenever you met someone new, it was always 'Oh, you are Solaja's daughter!' or 'So, you are Yomi's auntie's child!' or 'Ah, you are Mama Sola's mother's brother's granddaughter!'

In London, there is no giant tree. It's more like a giant fortress, with millions of people in separate cells behind their walls. Even the Community Centre has barbed wire here! The mentality is so different. I think the barbed wire gets into some people's brains. It's like they don't know the word RESPECT.

Monday 6th October

8 p.m.

I told Mariam about Papa and Mrs Wallace. I said, 'How would you feel if your mother married another man?' I thought she'd understand. But she laughed. She said that if the man was

102

rich enough for her mum not to have to work in her uncle's shop, it would be good. I told her it wasn't a joke. She said, 'I'm just being practical. Your dad probably likes this lady because he can talk with her about things. Don't be so jealous, Sade.' I was stunned. If I can't get even Mariam to understand my point of view, what's the use of trying to explain myself to anyone? When I'm talking to you, Iyawo, I know I'm only talking to myself.

CHAPTER 18

Terminator Eyebrows

At least fifteen people are reported to have been killed when a Nigerian fighter jet bombed the Military Headquarters of the Sierra Leone army in Freetown . . .

Papa's head stooped towards the little radio on the kitchen table. Femi dropped his rucksack by the door. Thud. Papa's eyes shot up, flicking from the floor to Femi. How stupid to be so casual with his school bag in front of Papa! That was asking for trouble. But Papa's eyes reverted to the radio, assuming a distant look as if he were thousands of miles away.

. . . The United Nations Security Council voted unanimously this week to impose international sanctions on Sierra Leone's military government. They include a ban on the sale of oil, weapons and military equipment . . .

Femi squeezed his fingers into his palms. The letter about Parents' Evening lay tucked in his bag. He was meant to have given it to Papa a week ago and today was the deadline for Papa's reply.

It hadn't worried him at first. Their form tutor, Miss Gray, was so scatty that he could always say he had handed in Papa's slip. She wouldn't be sure whether she had mislaid it and would simply ask him whether Papa was coming or not. But on Monday their Maths teacher, Ms Hassan, had walked into their tutor room and announced that Miss Gray was unwell. She would be their replacement form tutor 'for the foreseeable future'. She could have been carrying an invisible stun gun. So far no one in 7B had seriously messed around with Ms Hassan. After taking the register, she had opened a folder marked in bold letters:

7B PARENTS' EVENING
Tuesday 14th October

She had called out a list of names from a batch of reply slips. Those whose names were not called had to raise their hands. Femi's hand had felt like a lead weight. His plan was sunk.

Femi's eyes travelled from the bag to Papa and back again. The letter was still inside it. Whenever the thought had come into his mind that he shouldn't delay any longer, he had allowed it to slip away again. This morning was his last chance to give Papa the letter before having to account to Ms Hassan.

... A spokesman for the military government said that Sierra Leoneans should be free to sort out

their own problems without interference from Nigeria and the United Nations ...

If only he could be free of interference! The letter put him in a trap. If he gave it now, Papa would be mad at him for giving it so late. Papa liked to do things properly. He would say that he needed time to check that he could get away from work in time. But worse still, when Papa came to Parents' Evening, he would talk to Hendy and say something about football practice on Saturday afternoons. He would probably even start by thanking Hendy! Femi could just imagine the smile being wiped off Papa's face.

'Senseless! Brother killing brother!' Papa switched off the radio. The fury rumbled in his voice. Then he took a deep breath. He turned to Femi. 'Did you manage your homework last night?'

'Yes, Papa. It was easy.'

'What's easy?' Sade cut in from behind. She pressed past Femi into the kitchen. She already had her coat on.

'My homework!' Femi snapped.

'That's because you only do five minutes!'

'No I don't! You don't know because you play music in your room all the time!'

'Anyway, Papa will find out for himself when you have Parents' Evening. Haven't you got one yet?'

Femi froze. Trust Sade to bring up the subject! He was counting on her not knowing about arrangements for Year Seven.

'Stop quarrelling.' Papa rapped his fingers on the table. 'Don't you young people think we have enough wars already? You'll be late if you don't hurry up.'

Sade removed two packets of crisps from the

105

cupboard and held one out. Femi took it and unlatched his bag. As he stuffed the packet in, he glimpsed the letter for Papa tucked down the side. Suddenly he knew what to do.

'I'm ready! I've just got to get a book for science!' he called, darting back to his bedroom.

As soon as they reached school, Femi headed for the boys' cloakroom and into one of the cubicles. It was the most private place he knew in school. He sat down and pulled out his pen, the Parents' Evening letter and the *Dictionary of Science* that Papa had given him for his eleventh birthday. He balanced the book on his knees and spread out the letter on top of it. He focused on the bottom of the page.

```
I/We shall/shall not be able to attend Year Seven
Parents' Evening on Tuesday 14th October.

SIGNATURE OF PARENT/GUARDIAN ...
DATE ...
NAME OF CHILD ...
```

Carefully, he crossed out the words 'We shall'. He checked the sentence twice. 'I shall not be able to attend . . .' Now for the tricky part! His fingers flicked through the pages of the book until he pulled out a sheet of paper. Another letter. But this one was from Papa, written to his Year Six teacher at Greenslades Primary.

```
Dear Mr Fisher
I regret to inform you that Femi will not be able
to join his class on their outing to France.
```

Unfortunately the Home Office has still only granted us Temporary Admission. Without a proper travel document, Femi can go out of the country but he wouldn't be allowed back in. He is very upset to be missing this trip but I have done my best to explain the situation to him.

Yours sincerely

Folarin Solaja

Mr Fisher had told Femi he was very sorry and left Papa's letter lying on his desk. It was like an open sore and, when no one was looking, Femi had whisked it back. Reading the letter later in his bedroom, he felt empty. Without knowing why, he had hidden it between the pages of his *Dictionary of Science*. He couldn't have imagined then how it would be useful now. For a couple of moments he held his pen poised above the Parents' Evening letter. First he needed to practise. The margins in the top filled up with replicas of Papa's signature. Then he tore off the reply slip, printed the date and his name. The bell rang for registration. He mustn't be late for Ms Hassan. Taking the plunge, he signed: 'Folarin Solaja'.

Ms Hassan scanned the reply slip. Her brow puckered. Did she have X-ray eyes?

'Why can't your father come, Femi?'

He was caught in her spotlight.

'They won't let him have time off from work, miss.'

Her terminator eyebrows shot up.

'I am very surprised! I taught your sister last year. Your father never missed an opportunity to discuss her work.'

His stomach cramped.

'He says he'll come next time, miss, when I've been here longer.' Femi lowered his gaze.

Ms Hassan sighed loudly. 'The whole point . . .' She paused to get the attention of the class. 'The whole point of holding a Parents' Evening early in the term for first years is for us to spot problems before they become serious. It's for your own benefit.'

If he was wearing his hood, he would have let his head shrink away. He avoided looking around him as he returned to his seat. When Gary nudged him, he flinched like a snail. He didn't want to talk to anyone.

It was double bad luck that registration was followed by double Maths. The school had Papa's telephone number at the Refugee Centre. Was Ms Hassan suspicious enough to ring him? Whenever her eyes roamed in his direction, Femi wanted to duck. It was a miracle that he got through the lesson without her picking on him again.

At break, Femi said that he had a stomach-ache and had to get to the cloakroom. Gary offered to come with him.

'Nuh, man. I might be there all break!' he said irritably.

The stomach-ache was real, but instead of heading for the toilets, Femi weaved his way to the back of the school. He needed to see James. More to the point, he needed a puff on one of James's little roll-ups. There was a chance that James wouldn't be too pleased. He had made it quite clear that he didn't want Femi to be seen hanging around in school with him.

'Teachers like to think they're detectives, right. Two and two makes five and all that!' James had laughed, then turned serious. 'I want you to stay clean in school, you get my meaning?'

But hadn't James spoken briefly to Femi in school himself, once or twice? If he was careful not to be seen, Femi hoped that James wouldn't be mad at him for seeking him out now like an older brother.

Femi heard voices in the bicycle shed before he reached it. Approaching from the side, he couldn't see who was there and they couldn't see him either. But he could hear someone pleading. He held back behind the brick wall at the end of the shed.

'Please, man, I'm stressed out! Just a little, man! To see me through, right? I promise I'll –'

'No way. I don't do credit,' James cut in bluntly.

'I'll bring it to you tomorrow, man. Trust me!' The boy's voice rose to a whine.

'Nuh! Forget it! You already got me into trouble with Errol, bwoy! Never again, bwoy, never again!' James was beginning to heat up. 'Tomorrow is tomorrow. I deal today.'

Femi edged away from the wall. James was in no mood to be asked any favours. He had needed something to relax the tightness and cramps. This felt like a kick.

He hadn't meant to ask the question in front of Papa, but it popped out of his mouth at supper.

'What was Ms Hassan like when she taught you maths, Sade?'

Papa's spoon hovered in mid-air and his eyes lit up.

'Strict! Really strict!' His sister pulled a face. 'Ms

Hassan could teach in Nigeria! She doesn't let you get away with anything.'

'That just means she wants the best for her students,' Papa said. 'I hope you're not in trouble with her, Femi, eh?'

'No, Papa,' he mumbled.

'Good. When they have an evening for parents, I look forward to discussing your progress.'

Femi did not reply.

'Why are you asking about her?' Sade was about to turn detective.

'I just wanted to know. I like your pudding, Sade. You could be a chef.'

Thursday 9th October

9 p.m.

There's still a cloud between me and Papa. Mrs Wallace hasn't come here since Sunday and he has only mentioned her once. He was late for supper this evening because they had a meeting about refugees from Sierra Leone. From the way Papa said it, I could tell that he is still waiting for me to apologize. Luckily Femi interrupted. He doesn't usually bother asking about teachers, but he wanted to know about Ms Hassan. He's like a pressure cooker. Sometimes he is ready to explode and then, this evening, all his steam had escaped and he was quite nice to me. Papa said that he is looking forward to talking with Femi's teachers soon. Let's see what they have to say. If they aren't worried about him, why should I be?

P.S. I've been reading my last few entries, Iyawo. Maybe I've changed more than I want to admit. Mariam says I'm a lot tougher than I used to be. But then I think she is as well!

CHAPTER 19

Capture

The first thing Sade noticed as she opened the front door after school on Friday was Papa's briefcase.

'Why is Papa home so early?' Femi jostled her from behind.

Sade was about to say she wasn't psychic when she heard a female voice. Inside the living room Mrs Wallace was sitting next to the telephone with Papa's hand on her shoulder. Her spine was rigid, with her head bent over the receiver. Papa lifted a finger to his lips.

'The line is bad. Please repeat what you said . . .' Her voice was as stiff as her back. 'Rebels attacked Edward's school? . . . Abducted children, oh my God! What about Eddie? . . . No, I can't believe this, oh my God . . .'

Sade saw Papa's long fingers stretch over Mrs Wallace's shoulder. Her tone was rising.

'. . . Did no one try to stop them? What about the teachers, the police, the army? . . . Shot, my God! What's happening now? . . .' Mrs Wallace was shaking. Her free hand swung from her mouth to her fore-head, through her hair, out in front of her, beating the air, until Papa caught it and held it tight. Sade

111

watched, mesmerized. Femi stood stock-still beside her.

'I'm going to come! I have to . . . Of course I do. Yes, I know the risks . . . I know that, I know . . . All right, but . . . Does Mummy know? . . . I'll ring later . . .'

Papa signalled urgently to Mrs Wallace.

'Give your brother this number,' he whispered.

'You'd better take this number. It belongs to a friend . . .'

Mrs Wallace replaced the receiver. Slowly she lifted her face up to Papa. Although embarrassed by their intimacy, Sade didn't avert her eyes.

'Rebels broke into Eddie's dormitory – early this morning – a teacher tried to bar them – they shot him –' Mrs Wallace was breathing heavily. 'They forced twenty boys to go with them – at gunpoint – two escaped but – but –' She was struggling to string her words together in a whirlwind. 'But Eddie is missing. My Eddie – is – miss–'

Her words dissolved into sobs. Strange, alarming adult sobs that swept Sade back to a room full of shocked grown-ups and Mama's sister wailing over their mother's body wrapped in an embroidered bedspread, drenched in crimson. For the second time in a week, Sade saw Papa enclose Mrs Wallace in his arms. Sade fled to her room.

She lay on top of her bed with her headphones on and music drowning all sound from the living room. But pictures, already seeded inside her head, insisted on unfurling themselves. The images would have been like a story in a film if she hadn't seen those children talking to Auntie Hannah. Real, flesh-and-blood children talking about doing things so frightful that no child would make them up. Their blank eyes spoke the truth. She had no idea what Edward looked like. But a face emerged like a photo-fit with two terrified black holes for eyes and a gaping slash for a mouth. It belonged to a boy being grabbed from his bed. A boy in pyjamas with a rifle poking him in the back, trampling over the body of his teacher, stumbling barefoot across a schoolyard before disappearing into thick dark forest. What would the rebels do to him? What would they make him do?

Sade returned to the kitchen when it was time to prepare supper. Through the doorway she heard Papa ring the cab office and cancel his work for the night. Mrs Wallace sat with her face covered by her hands. The tall, upright figure suddenly looked reduced and vulnerable. Sade left her headphones hanging around her neck and worked in silence. She washed the rice slowly, her fingers sifting through the grains in the cloudy water. An urgent conversation was beginning next door.

'Don't rush, Cynthie, please. You – we – need to think this through. They could arrest you the moment you land in Freetown.'

'I'll have to take the risk. I'll tell them, I'm not coming back to disturb their sleep with my articles. I'm coming back to look for my son!'

'Eh, eh! We can't expect soldiers to be rational! If they lock you up – what good is that to Edward and your family? They will have two people to worry about!'

Sade's mind somersaulted. Before they had fled to England, it was Papa who had taken risks – and he was the one who had to be cautioned by Uncle Tunde.

They're not finished with you, Folarin! . . . They won't

stop until they've shut you up . . . Tell me, what can you write from the grave?

Now here was Papa trying to convince Mrs Wallace to be careful! Reminding her of danger. The government soldiers would laugh in her face. Why should they care if the son of a troublesome 'pen pusher' had been kidnapped by rebels? They might say this should teach her a lesson. Papa spoke bluntly and Mrs Wallace said less and less.

'You don't have to make a decision tonight. There are things we can do here. We'll contact the International Red Cross – give them a photo of Edward. We'll alert aid workers in the camps to look out for him.'

There was silence. Sade glanced into the living room. Mrs Wallace was staring blankly ahead, not looking at Papa. With the film that must be running in her head, probably she could not even hear him.

Mrs Wallace barely touched her plate of rice and beans. After supper, she made another call to Freetown. From the snatches Sade heard, it sounded as if Mrs Wallace's brother was saying the same things as Papa. Afterwards, when Mrs Wallace wanted to return to her lodgings, Papa was adamant. She should not spend the night alone. He would sleep on the sofa in the living room so she could have his bedroom.

'Mrs Wallace can have my bed, Papa. I'll sleep on the sofa. I'm shorter than you.' The words came out of Sade's mouth before she had even thought about what she was saying.

'Thank you, Sade,' Mrs Wallace accepted quietly. She sounded exhausted. 'If I can sleep, maybe I shall think more clearly in the morning.'

If Papa was surprised, he kept it to himself. She had

114

surprised herself. As she returned to her room to take what she needed for the night, she wondered what had come over her. She noticed that Femi's door was already closed. No point trying to talk to him. She hadn't heard him say a single word since the phone call from Freetown.

Friday 10th October

Midnight (Living room, not my bedroom)

I've been trying to sleep for two hours but I can't. It's my own fault. I am stuck like a giant on our tiny sofa because I offered Mrs Wallace my bed. Unbelievable but true. Armed rebels in Sierra Leone have kidnapped her son with some other boys from his school! When I offered my bed, I couldn't believe my own ears! Maybe it's guilt because I've kept wishing her to disappear and leave Papa alone. But I would never have wanted it to happen this way. Especially not after seeing those children who talked to Aunt Hannah. Mrs Wallace usually looks like a forceful person but tonight she was scared and helpless. It must be one of the worst feelings in the world. It's not only that her son is in danger but the rebels will make him do brutal, cruel things. Just imagine if Femi was in boarding school far away and something like this happened to him??? The things I've been worrying about don't seem so bad now. As Mama used to say: 'You won't complain of burnt porridge if your house is on fire.'

CHAPTER 20

If

Femi lay awake for a long time after he turned off his bedroom light. He didn't know what Edward Wallace looked like, but he imagined a neat face with mischievous eyes and a toothy grin. What was it like to be asleep in your dormitory and to be woken by screams and gunshots? What was it like to be force-marched into the bush? If the trees were as thick as the forest around Family Home where Grandma lived, there would be such a tangle of branches that the rebels would have to carry machetes as well as guns. Edward was only twelve, like him. Had he been allowed to put on his shoes and proper clothes? Or were the boys forced out barefoot and in their pyjamas? What would happen if a boy was too tired to walk any more? Sade had told him about Aunt Hannah's interviews when he had been helping her dry the dishes earlier in the week.

You can't imagine what brutal things those boys were made to do, Femi.

She had refused to give him all the details.

You would have nightmares.

Sade always thought she knew best. He tossed and turned. Then suddenly it struck him. If Papa was going to be so involved with Mami Cynthie and this business over Edward, he wouldn't have time for anything else. There was no need to worry about Ms Hassan and Parents' Evening after all.

When Femi came down for his cornflakes on Saturday morning, Mami Cynthie was already at the kitchen table with Papa. Her face was like one of those sad masks on the wall in Papa's study at home in Lagos, but she looked calmer than the previous night. She had spoken again to her brother in Freetown and he had persuaded her not to travel out yet. He had promised to do everything he could to find out where Edward and the other boys had been taken. Even if they were found, it would be very dangerous for the army to storm their camp. The boys would be made to fight and could be killed.

'People in Britain need to know what's going on,' said Papa. 'They respond to personal stories. They'll want their government to do more. UN sanctions aren't enough to get a ceasefire.'

Femi listened as Papa spoke about Mami Cynthie taking Edward's story to the newspapers. But his attention drifted when they began to talk about a Commonwealth Conference. Pressing his cornflakes into the milk, he wondered what James was planning for today. His ears pricked up at mention of Aunt Hannah. If Papa and Mama Cynthie were busy meeting her and other journalists, that gave him more freedom. He waited for a break in the conversation to ask for money for swimming. Papa pulled out some coins from his pocket.

'I want you to be especially considerate of your sister today,' said Papa. 'She didn't get much sleep last night.'

117

'Yes, Papa.'

His father must have heard him moaning at Sade to hurry up in the bathroom a little earlier.

'Do you have football practice this afternoon?'

Papa leant forward to observe him over the rim of his glasses. Femi bobbed his head.

'I'm glad,' said Papa. 'That'll keep you busy.'

Mama Cynthie was pressing her lips together as if to smile, but Femi saw that she was also fighting back tears. He withdrew into finishing his cornflakes.

CHAPTER 21

'Keep walking, little brother'

Approaching the Leisure Centre, he was surprised to see James already waiting there. Alone. Tapping his foot. Even from a distance, Femi felt uneasy.

'Keep walking, little brother.' James swung his arm around Femi's shoulder and turned him ninety degrees. Femi struggled to keep pace with James's long strides. They were heading back towards the High Street.

'Errol wants you. Urgent, right.'

'Where's everyone else?' Femi raised his voice to make himself heard above the Saturday morning traffic.

'Busy.' James wasn't forthcoming. As soon as James removed his arm, Femi moved aside to let oncoming pedestrians between them. When the whole gang walked together, it was other people who always gave way. Each time a bus passed by from the direction of his estate, he ducked his head. If Papa was in one of them with Mami Cynthie, he would want to know what Femi was doing walking in the opposite direction to the Leisure Centre. The High Street was much more exposed than the shopping precinct where the gang usually hung out.

Femi was about to turn away from the next oncoming bus when the roar of a car engine drowned out all other noise. A sunflower-yellow car with a black top was hurtling towards the bus from behind, dangerously claiming the road. It overtook just as the bus trundled past Femi and James. It was a BMW, like the one that had picked up Errol the previous week. Femi swivelled round to catch a glimpse of its occupants. But the bus obscured his view and, by the time he saw it again, it was too far away. Probably it was the same car.

'Does that belong to Errol's friends?' he asked. James didn't reply and Femi decided not to repeat his question. James's urgency made him uneasy. He secretly hoped that the BMW had whisked Errol away again.

James led Femi to the back room in the garage. Two young men came out as they entered. Errol was stretched out on the armchair with his feet on the box table. He would have looked relaxed if it hadn't been for the way he drummed his fingers on the armrest.

'Sit down, Femi bwoy,' he commanded.

Femi balanced precariously on the edge of a box.

119

He felt Errol's eyes secure him from behind the dark glasses.

'I want you to do something for me,' Errol said. 'I want you to do it just like I say, right. No messing. You get it?'

'Sure, Errol,' Femi said hastily.

Errol's fingers dipped into the front pocket of his jacket and pulled out a small parcel. It was not the shape of the parcel Femi had taken to Sade. This one was smaller and squarish, wrapped in white plastic. Errol leant forward and positioned it on the table gently, as if it were delicate glass. His fingers returned to his pocket and this time he fished out a piece of paper.

'D'you know this place?'

Femi squinted. 51 DURRANT COURT. That was the block of flats at the far end of the same estate where he lived. Worried that his voice might tremble, he nodded.

'Good. I want you to deliver this packet. They'll give you an envelope. It'll be sealed, right. You don't open it. Just bring it back, no chatting on the way, no delay. Simple, yeah?'

Again he nodded. He was biting the inside of his lip.

Errol turned sharply to James. 'What's wrong with this little brother of yours? He's lost his voice. You sure he's not a chicken?'

'He's safe,' James asserted. 'Right, Femi?'

'Yeah . . . right.' Femi heard the small voice as if it belonged to someone else.

Errol stroked the rings on his left hand with his right forefinger. 'If my brother here says you're safe, I take his word.' His eyes never left Femi. 'One more thing. I want no chirping later. Everything stays inside this room. You get my meaning?'

'Yeah.' This time he tried to sound more confident. He stretched out for the packet and slipped it into the inside pocket of his anorak. The movement was a little too quick, awkward.

Errol suddenly burst out laughing.

'You're not a chicken, nuh! That's 'cause you look like a squirrel! But where's the bushy tail, right?'

Femi's eyes darted to James. He was grinning as well. Femi tried to force a smile.

'Maybe they don't have squirrels in Nigeria,' said James.

'We have bush rats.' He should have kept quiet.

'Bush rats! They eat them, yeah?' Errol thrust the question at him. Was this another snare? Despite Papa's boyhood tales of the pleasures of catching and roasting the animals in the bush near Family Home, Femi had always felt squeamish.

'Some people like the meat,' he mumbled.

'That's nature, right? If the rat was bigger, he'd eat the man . . .' Errol paused as if he wanted Femi to take some bigger meaning. 'Well, what you waiting for? I want you back here chop-chop.'

Femi lurched to his feet. The fingers of his left hand squeezed the small package inside his pocket. They were sweating and he hadn't even begun his mission. He looked across the box table at James.

'Get moving, little brother. You heard what Errol said. It's dead easy. No one will take notice of a kid.'

James wasn't coming with him. He was on his own.

CHAPTER 22

'No one will take notice of a kid'

He had to pass his own block to reach Durrant Court. That meant not being spotted by his family or everything would collapse like a pack of cards. With his head sunk into his anorak hood, he jogged off through the shortcut. He jostled with reasons for visiting Durrant Court instead of being in the Leisure Centre. Could he say a friend had hurt himself in the swimming pool and he was running to tell the friend's mother? But the attendants would have rung her, wouldn't they? He could say that the phone was broken. But what if Papa wanted to come with him to Durrant Court? Even if Papa was occupied with Mami Cynthie, he might insist that Sade should go with him.

The overgrown path and the half-finished houses were behind him now. He was out in the open and the first of the grey concrete blocks, his own, loomed ahead. Durrant Court was the fourth and last. There was only one solution. Not to be caught. He put his head down and pelted along the estate road, raising his hood just enough to see where he was going. The panic-stricken butterflies in his stomach had turned into a herd of elephants. As long as he could get past his own block without being stopped, he would be OK. If Papa or Sade called him from behind, he could always pretend he hadn't heard. When he returned, it would be too late for them to check on his injured-friend story.

It was a marvel he didn't knock into anyone. He dodged some children playing with bikes. They swore at him for crashing through their game and, seconds later, a peevish woman's voice called out a warning. He didn't see any of their faces, only bicycle wheels, legs and the woman's stick. But no one shouted his name. When he reached the entrance to Durrant Court, he pulled to a halt at the bottom of the stairs next to the lift, breathing heavily. He needed to recover. He had been so anxious about getting here that he hadn't even thought about his mission. It sounded simple. Go to Number 51. Ask for Julie. Hand over the packet and collect the envelope at the same time. Don't ask questions. Take it back to Errol.

He pressed the button for the lift. It wheezed and groaned as it descended. At least it was working. The lift in their block was out of order most of the time. The lift arrived, clanking and rattling. The door swung open and four men peeled out. Femi felt their stares as if he were being X-rayed. They looked similar to the young men who hung around with Errol: apparently casual, but with wary, probing eyes. Instinctively Femi patted his anorak with his left hand, feeling the package in the inside pocket. He immediately regretted it. He might give away that he had something to protect. He swung the offending hand to the lift door and stepped inside. The awful smell almost gagged him as the door closed. He wanted to dive out and use the stairs. But the men remained in a huddle, eyeing him through the glass panel. They unnerved him. Instead, he threw one hand over his nose and mouth and pressed the button for the fifth floor with the other. As the lift cranked itself up, he glimpsed the faces crack into smiles.

Flat 51 was at the far end of the corridor. As long as no one came out from one of the red doors on his right, he would be all right now. He wanted no more encounters. The exchange should take less than a minute, and he would be on his way. The sooner this was over, the better. It would be a relief to be back with the gang in the shopping precinct. Those expeditions still made his heart beat fast but at least there were others with him. Afterwards they would have a laugh and reward themselves with sweets, snacks, whatever they chose. He hadn't dared ask if Errol would give him anything when he returned.

The bell at 51 chimed brightly. It was followed by silence. Femi pressed again. Chime. Silence . . . Chime. Silence. A boa constrictor was now gathering itself around his chest. What should he do if there was no one here? Would he have to go all the way back to explain? Errol might tell him to repeat the journey! Femi clenched his fist and knocked at the door. He felt like hammering on it, but that might bring out the neighbours. This Julie person had to be in!

At last he heard shuffling, then a chain being removed. The door edged open and a painfully thin white woman examined him for a moment before signalling him urgently to come in. She was wearing a shiny pink dressing gown and slippers. With ashen skin, hollow cheeks and bruise-like shadows under milky blue eyes, she looked ill.

'You don't want to wake the whole block,' she complained. 'Close the door and give me my stuff!'

They were standing in the narrow hallway. She was blocking the entrance to the living room and was so close that he could smell her breath.

'Are you J–?'

Femi stopped just in time, remembering his instructions.

'What's your name?' he asked, hot with embarrassment. Asking a grown-up a question like that still sounded so rude. Thank goodness she wasn't an African lady. He might never have got the question out.

'Of course I'm Julie. I could've died waiting. Give me the packet!'

'Errol says you've got to give me an envelope.'

'You'll get it. Show me what you brought. Got to check it's the right stuff first!' The woman, Julie, grasped Femi's anorak sleeve and pulled him towards her. He lost his balance and they both stumbled. They would have fallen if it hadn't been for the wall. Femi steadied himself, able now to see into the living room. His eyes swung across a worn settee with crumpled cushions to a low glass table littered with dirty plates, mugs, teaspoons and a cigarette lighter. His gaze fixed on a clutter of needles. It looked like the kind of mess they sometimes found in the stairwell of their block of flats. He felt sick.

The more Julie pleaded and harangued, the less he said and the more he tried to retreat inside his hood. He wanted to get out of here but he had to follow Errol's instructions.

125

Give her the packet when she gives you the envelope.

He hadn't asked Errol what was in either of them. He hadn't wanted to know. If he just followed the instructions, everything would be OK.

'All right! I'll get it!' At last Julie was going to give him the envelope. 'It was here a moment ago!' She scoured the mantelpiece, the table with the needles, the settee. She threw aside the loose cushions, then pulled up the seats. She was becoming frantic, cursing Femi and everything else.

'What's wrong, Mum?' A girl's voice cut in behind Femi. It sounded irritated. His hood stopped his side vision so he had to turn his head completely to see the speaker. The moment he did, he regretted it. It was Marcia's friend Donna, the one who had been at Errol's house. Her small blue eyes, sunk behind black oval lines and white cheeks, were sizing him up. She put her hand on her hip. 'Oooh, Sade's brother, right? What d'you want?'

As if she didn't know!

'You know what he's come for! Help me!' Donna's mother was kneeling on the floor, scattering a pile of magazines, close to tears. She sounded more of a child than her daughter.

'All right, all right, Mum! Have you looked in the kitchen?'

'Look for me, please, love!' Julie whimpered. She was rocking, trying to stop quivering. She squeezed herself until her knuckles were taut and white and the veins on her hand looked like chicken's claws. Femi stood, mesmerized. Donna strode into the kitchen. Seconds later she reappeared, waving a brown envelope like a fan.

126

'Give it to him, love! Get my stuff!' Julie was pushing up her gown sleeve. Her scrawny arm was covered with a grille of crazy lines. Donna swiped the envelope past Femi's face and held it just out of his reach.

'Where's my mum's thingy then?'

Femi thrust the packet towards her, grabbed the envelope and fled.

Sprinting along the open corridor, with the brown envelope safely inside his anorak pocket, Femi didn't care that it had started to rain. At least he could breathe out here. He wouldn't use the foul-smelling lift. Instead he bounded down the stairs. The rain also meant that there was less chance of being noticed on his return journey. In fifteen minutes he would be back at the garage, home and dry.

They caught him at ground level. Three pairs of hands grabbed him and the fourth held open the door to the lift. Compressed by bodies, he was submerged, begging for air. Harsh voices demanded that he empty his pockets, but his hands were trapped. Strong, bony fingers crawled over him, poking, prodding. They wrenched open his anorak. In less than a second, the brown envelope was once again waving in front of him. A quick slitting of paper and there was laughter. Femi glimpsed the wodge of pinky-brown notes. Tens or twenties? Was it one hundred, two hundred, more? He began to struggle, to plead.

'It's not mine! Give it back! Please!'

Hopeless. A rough hand smothered his face, squeezing his jaw between thumb and fingers. Each of his wrists was seized in a vice, his right arm twisted up his back. The pain screamed through him but the gag over his mouth forced it back, swirling inside him. No air. He was crumbling, crashing.

Alone on the floor of the lift, Femi gasped for breath. He wanted to vomit but the effort would exhaust him. Afterwards he would have to lie there. Someone would find him. There would be Questions. If he told anyone that he had been robbed of so much money, they would want to know where he had got it from. Errol would never, never forgive him. As it was, what was Errol going to say to him? Do to him? Errol would already be wondering why he hadn't returned. What if Errol didn't believe him? What if he thought Femi had taken the money himself and made up a story about being mugged?

Head throbbing, Femi forced himself up. He leant on the door and reeled out of the lift. Beyond the entrance, the rain was tossing down now. He ran outside, floundering, not bothering to avoid the puddles on the uneven tarmac. The harder the rain beat down on him, the fiercer he imagined Errol's fury would be.

Saturday 11th October

2.15 p.m.

Femi has come home in a TERRIBLE state. Soaked. Shuddering. He staggered to the bathroom, collapsed by the toilet and was sick. His face wasn't just wet from the rain. He was crying. When he stopped vomiting, I told him to have a hot shower and put on dry clothes. When I took him a cup of tea, he was under his duvet, still shivering. I begged him to tell me what had happened. Had someone beaten him up? Was it something to do with James or Lizard

128

Eyes? He rolled away from me and wouldn't say anything. So I said I would have to tell Papa. That made him hysterical. He yelled that I would make everything worse and Papa could end up getting killed! I told him he shouldn't say things like that. But when I asked what he meant, he clammed up. He was fighting tears and he turned his back on me again. There was no point going on at him so I reminded him about his tea and left.

It's staring me in the face that I <u>should</u> have told Papa long ago. I kept making excuses not to. But if something bad happens to Femi now, Papa will never forgive me and I will never forgive myself.

CHAPTER 23

Flaring Tempers, Flashing Metal

Femi tried to bury himself under his duvet. It was three hours since Errol had sent him to Durrant Court. The longer he stayed away, the worse it would be. Errol would come after him, send someone for him. James knew where he lived and he would tell Errol. He called Femi 'little brother', but he had also warned him that Errol was unforgiving. The men in the BMW – Errol's friends – wouldn't stand for being messed around.

Femi's mind twisted and turned. He should have gone to the garage right away. Errol would have seen the state he was in and been angry that the muggers attacked someone from his gang. If he didn't know them himself, his friends would. They must know everyone on the estate. Errol's friends would find them and get the money back. How stupid of him to have run home! There was much less chance of Errol listening to him now. Maybe Errol's taunts were right. He was chicken. If he didn't get to the garage soon and sort it out, the trouble would spill over. Papa would get to know. That was unthinkable. He had to go and speak to Errol before it was too late.

Femi crept into the corridor, thankful to hear music coming from Sade's room. It would help cover his footsteps. He tiptoed into the bathroom and lifted his anorak off the curtain rail where Sade had hung it up to dry. Carrying his coat, still wet, he tiptoed past her door. It was slightly open and she was writing at her desk, with her back to him. From this angle, her face almost seemed to be touching her Iyawo head. He turned the latch to the front door as softly as possible and slipped out.

It was no longer raining, but the air was grey and damp as he raced through the shortcut, trying to rehearse what he should say. When he saw James leaning against the garage wall, he felt a wave of relief. Errol must still be inside and James could be a mediator. But as soon as he was close enough to see James's face, he remembered the voice in the bicycle shed. Hard. Cold. The voice that had refused to help a pleading boy.

'What time d'you call this, bwoy? I vouched for you! Look how you mess me up. Let's see how you like the heat!' James signalled for him to go inside. Femi had no time to explain anything before entering the fire. James stepped behind him, blocking any retreat.

The two young men whom he had seen earlier that morning shifted out as soon as he entered. This time, he knew: they were on sentry duty. Errol sprang up from his armchair and stood with his arms folded, legs apart. There was only the box table between them, and Errol towered above him.

'What have you got for me?' The eyes behind the dark glasses pinned him down but not the million butterflies in his stomach.

'I – I – I haven't got it, Errol! Four – four men mugged me! They forced me into the lift! I put the envelope here!' Femi thrust open his anorak and showed Errol the empty pocket. 'I – I'm telling the truth, Errol, I promise – no – please, Errol – no!'

With a single stride Errol closed in on Femi, kicking the box table aside and gripping Femi's wrist, twisting and turning him. The pain pierced where he was already tender.

'You think I stupid, Mister African bwoy! Why you take so long coming back, heh? You ran home, right? My friends saw you. You ran home to hide my money, right?'

'No, it's not true! I went home 'cause I was going to be sick! I've been vomiting!' Femi howled. 'Ask my s–!' He stopped. If Errol said anything to Sade, it would get to Papa. But Errol had already guessed what he was going to say and it seemed to increase his fury. He accused Femi of cheating him, of being as stuck up as his sister Sade, of needing a lesson.

'Tell him I'm not like that!' Femi entreated James. 'I never cheated! Tell him!' Errol's knee was pressing on a nerve in his back and the muscles in his arms felt as if they were ripping apart. Through his tears he saw James looking deadpan, silent.

With an unexpected yank, Errol readjusted his hold. One arm swooped like a lasso around Femi's trunk. The other swirled up with a vicious glint and a blade grazed past Femi's face. He butted his head away but was barricaded by Errol's chest.

'Cool it, brother, cool it! He's only a kid. He wouldn't cheat you.'

James was coming to the rescue, at last. But, to Femi's horror, the words were like a match. Suddenly Errol was bawling accusations at James. Maybe he was behind Femi! Maybe he was cheating on him! Maybe he had cheated him over Sade too! Errol's knife quivered in front of Femi.

Femi didn't know who lunged first but he saw the blade slice across James's chin and a spray of blood arch towards him. In the wrench and tussle that followed, Errol released his clutch and Femi hurtled on to the armchair. The armrest splintered beneath him, breaking away from the chair. He grabbed one end of the L-shaped baton and edged towards the door. James and Errol were wheezing heavily, each locked around the other as James struggled for the knife. He was trying to say something. It was a grunt but it sounded to Femi like 'Run!'

What happened next was a blur. A flare of metal and a tangle of jerking elbows, arms, hands. James was sinking, plummeting. Femi brandished the broken armrest, ready to beat his way out past the sentries. But they propelled themselves into the room so rapidly that they didn't notice him beside the door. Femi took his chance. As he fled, an image flicked past the corner of his eye. One of the sentries was tugging something out from inside his jacket. Femi was already halfway across the forecourt when a shot detonated his mind and sent him plunging down the High Street.

CHAPTER 24

The Story Tumbles Out

Sade woke with the sound of voices. Papa and Mrs Wallace were back. She glanced at the little clock beside Iyawo. Quarter past four. Her magazine had slipped off her bed. She must have fallen asleep. If Femi had also napped, he might have calmed down a little. She would ask him one more time to talk to Papa himself. Otherwise it would be up to her. If Papa thought he only had Mrs Wallace to worry about, he was in for a shock. There was a saying for it . . .

Just because you are running from the jaws of the crocodile, do you think the leopard will let you pass?

Sade knocked on Femi's door, softly, then louder. When there was no reply, she opened it and saw his duvet piled up on his bed. No Femi. But it was only when she saw that his anorak was no longer hanging on the rail in the bathroom that her heart slipped. She hurried to the living room, calling his name.

'What's wrong, Sade? Femi should be at football

practice, eh?' Papa poked his head out of the kitchen.

'No, Papa – he was here! I don't know where he's gone!'

Mrs Wallace appeared behind Papa. Sade averted her eyes as she forced the story to tumble out, starting with the terrified state in which Femi had come home earlier. The tale was like a jigsaw with a gaping hole in the centre. She wanted to leave out the messages that Lizard Eyes had sent her, her suspicions about James, her futile attempt to get James to lay off Femi. But they could all be clues. Papa let her speak without interruption. When she finished, she stared at her clasped palms, waiting for an onslaught of questions and reproach. Instead she felt a heavy silence.

Truth keeps the hand cleaner than soap.

Her hands were deeply muddied.

'Have you any idea where these boys might be?' Papa's low voice shook like distant thunder.

Sade glanced up. His face was etched with dismay.

'No, Papa. That Errol Richards sometimes waits outside school. Sometimes he hangs round the shops in the High Street but I've never seen him on our estate.'

Papa was already pulling on his coat.

'I'm going to the cab office – see if I can get a cab – I'll check the school, High Street, Leisure Centre, the estate, everywhere.'

'Shall I come with you, Folarin?' Mrs Wallace asked quietly.

'No. Please stay here with Sade. If Femi returns, he'll need you.'

The words pierced Sade with guilt. It was so clear now. By keeping quiet all these weeks, she had been totally irresponsible. To top it all – today – when she

134

knew Femi was in trouble, she had taken a nap and let him escape. How could Papa trust her any more? Instead he had to ask for help from Mrs Wallace, who was already sick with worry about her own son.

Sade answered the phone just before six o'clock.
'Is Femi back?'
'No, Papa.'
There was a moment's silence.
'I'm going to the police.'

CHAPTER 25

Arrest

Femi crouched on the seat, his head in his hands scrunched above his knees. He was tense, stiff, aching. No one else had been in the cloakroom when he had hurtled into the end cubicle. With luck, no one had noticed that the door had not been opened for hours. He glanced at his watch. Quarter to ten. What would happen at closing time? Would the attendants check that they weren't locking anyone in? He couldn't imagine spending a night alone in the Leisure Centre, yet where else could he go? He couldn't face Papa with blood spattered down his shirt! What if Papa had gone to the police? If the police found him, they would want to know about the blood. If he told them what Errol had done to James, he would be dead meat if Errol ever caught him.

Errol's words reminded him of a small gazelle, caught in the headlights of Papa's car on the road to Grandma's village and Family House. Papa didn't like to drive at night, but they had been delayed and he was driving fast. *Move! Shift!* They had all willed the wide-eyed, petrified animal to run, but it had turned to look at the car and stopped, right there in the middle of the road. By the time Papa had tried to brake, it was too late. 'Paralysed with fright.' That's what Papa had said. Femi still remembered the dull, sickening thud. That was the first time he had thought about death.

The picture of James collapsing at Errol's feet kept returning. What if Errol had killed him? The shot still echoed in his head. Was it just a car backfiring or was it from a gun? What if James had been left wounded, bleeding to death? James had acted the big brother. He had tried to protect Femi from Errol's fury. But he, Femi, had been such a coward that he hadn't even tried to call an ambulance. What kind of little brother was that?

Every time the cloakroom door opened, Femi drew in his breath. Full alert. As soon as the news got around, the whole gang would turn against him. They would think he had stolen the money, got James involved – and then deserted him. They might even guess that he was in the Leisure Centre. The toilets were an obvious place. With a leg-up, someone could look over the top of the cubicle. They would find a way of getting him out. He had nothing with which he could protect himself. Only a broken piece of wood from Errol's armchair.

*

Shortly after ten, the cloakroom door was thrust open, followed by shuffling and heavy footsteps. It sounded like an army. Femi jolted up on to his feet and squeezed himself into the back corner of the cubicle, gripping the armrest close to his stomach. A swift shadow above him cut out the light. By the time he looked up, it had gone. He had been identified.

'Femi Solaja, we're police. We've seen your photograph. Your father has been to see us. He's very worried about you.' It was a woman's voice, calm and steady.

Femi gritted his teeth. Why had Papa sent the police? They would see the blood!

'A boy was seriously attacked this afternoon. We need to speak to you. If you have any weapons, slide them under the door right away.'

How did the police know that he had anything to do with James? Papa couldn't have told them! Femi pressed his back harder against the wall, trying to stop himself shaking.

'Do you hear me, Femi?'

He heard all right. Like the wide-eyed gazelle had seen Papa's car.

'If you have any weapons, push them under the door now.'

Weapons? Surely they couldn't mean this splintered piece of wood? They meant the knife jabbing up and down into James. They meant the gun with the shot still resounding in his head.

'If you don't respond, Femi, my armed colleagues will have to bring you out.'

It was a no-nonsense voice. It expected to be obeyed. But it was on the other side of the door and Errol's voice was closer, circling inside his head . . .

Say anything, boy, and you're dead meat, you under-stand?

He could see Errol's dark glasses targeting him. Femi shut his eyes. Seconds later, all hell broke loose.

'PUT YOUR WEAPON ON THE FLOOR! WEAPON ON THE FLOOR! PUSH IT UNDER THE DOOR! UNDER THE DOOR!'

The screams hit him with such terrifying force that his fingers released the armrest. It clattered to the floor.

'. . . UNDER THE DOOR!'

His foot kicked the wood and it spun across the cubicle, under the door, out of sight.

'PUT ALL YOUR WEAPONS DOWN! PUSH THEM OUT NOW! NOW!'

His head was splitting. He didn't have any other weapons.

'OPEN THE DOOR SLOWLY AND SHOW ME THE PALMS OF YOUR HANDS! THE PALMS OF YOUR HANDS!'

He jerked to the door like a puppet. His fingers fumbled with the latch. His left hand gripped the door, inching around the edge. For a couple of seconds longer the door was his shield. He thrust out his right palm.

'COME OUT SLOWLY WITH YOUR HANDS WHERE WE CAN SEE THEM! HANDS ON YOUR HEAD! ON YOUR HEAD!'

He let go of the door and raised his hands, so petrified that his tears were frozen. Three rifles pointed at him from close range. Three men in black followed every move. Behind them, to the right, more police stood by the cloakroom door.

'GET DOWN ON THE FLOOR! FACE DOWN! ON THE FLOOR!'

The screaming was as loud as if Femi was at the far end of a football field. Femi threw himself down beneath the rifles.

'ARMS SPREAD OUT! OUT!'

Splayed out, he felt someone pounce and pull his wrists behind his back. They were snapped together, tight. Skin-biting tight. Hands padded down his legs, hips, trunk, everywhere. Someone was checking the toilet where he had hidden. Then he was being hauled up, dusted down. A hand was unzipping his anorak.

'Ah! What have we here?' The man in black who had been yelling lowered his voice. It was suddenly ordinary but his face was the colour of over-ripe pawpaw. Femi looked down. The splashes on his grey sweatshirt were an even deeper red than the man's face. Three new police officers now closed in on him. Femi saw their eyes fix on the bloodstains.

'No gun, Sergeant. No knife. Only this.' The broken armrest lay awkwardly near Femi's feet. The officer pulled a pair of small scissors from his pocket and swivelled Femi around.

'Over to you now, Sarge,' he said as he snipped the cuffs.

A plastic strip fell to the floor. Femi rubbed his wrists.

'What's this blood about?'

This was the same firm female voice that had spoken to him before the yeller. A finger whirled in front of his sweatshirt, but Femi avoided looking up.

'There's been a very nasty assault near by,' the policewoman continued evenly. 'You fit the description and you've got blood on your clothes. I'm arresting you on suspicion of being involved –'

I'm arresting you. He didn't hear anything else.

They led him out of the Leisure Centre towards their van with a police officer on either side of him and one behind. It was when he saw the cage inside the back of the van that he panicked and tried to wriggle away. They grabbed him easily but he struggled and kicked until they pinned him down. When Femi looked up, he was surprised to realize that the hands holding him in an iron grip were those of the policewoman. This time they handcuffed him with metal cuffs, his arms in front. He fought back his tears as he scrambled up the steps. There were two seats inside the cage facing each other. He sat on one as the cage door was locked, then the van door locked. As the vehicle juddered into motion, he gripped the wire with his fingers and buried his head in the crook of his arm.

Saturday 11th October

11.30 p.m.

THE POLICE HAVE GOT FEMI. They rang Papa half an hour ago to say he must bring Femi clean clothes. What does that mean???

When Papa went to the police station earlier, the desk lady wrote a few details and told Papa to go home. She said hundreds of children go missing every year and come back when they are hungry. But Papa refused to go until a detective came to talk to him. When Papa described Femi, the detective suddenly wanted Femi's school photo. He said there was a serious attack on a boy this afternoon and a boy fitting Papa's description of Femi was seen running away!!! Papa came back from the police station looking like a ghost.

Mrs Wallace made supper tonight. I didn't feel like eating but Papa insisted I join them. He made me go over everything I'd already told him. He double-checked everything, as if I might still be hiding some of the truth. Then, when the police rang to say they had Femi, Papa told me to get Femi's clothes. I pulled out a brand new red T-shirt from one of Femi's drawers that I've never seen before. Papa came into the room and saw it too. He frowned and said, 'Not that one.' Nothing else.

I feel so dreadful, Iyawo. Papa has gone to the police station and Mrs Wallace is staying again tonight even though I told Papa I'd be all right on my own. She's alone in our living room, watching a film. She must be trying to take her mind off Edward and now Femi. She asked me if I wanted to watch it with her. I said I was going to bed. I know I won't be able to sleep until Papa brings Femi back. It's icy cold in my room even though I'm sitting under my duvet with my clothes on. I've been thinking of the night the police raided our house in Lagos. They seized Papa's articles, papers and passport and forced him into the back of their truck. After we had cleared up the mess, Femi and I cuddled up with Mama on the sofa. We watched television until the TV station shut down. We were all very frightened, but at least we still felt like a family.

CHAPTER 26

Murder?

Femi stood, surrounded by black-and-white uniforms, in front of the raised desk at the centre of a large room. Every time he shifted his arms, the handcuffs pinched his skin. On one side was a corridor lined with metal doors and, above him, at least two cameras in the ceiling. The custody sergeant behind the desk had his own camera eyes. They kept scanning the room as well as darting back and forth between Femi and the computer. He tapped the keyboard as the policewoman reported the charge. This time Femi heard the words: '. . . arrested on suspicion of being involved in a serious assault . . .'

Once again, instead of listening properly to what followed, his head throbbed. *James was alive.* 'Serious assault' meant that James wasn't dead.

He wanted to retreat into his shell, but there was more prodding and probing. Hands searched him again. When they found nothing, the handcuffs were removed and he was told to take off his shoes, then empty his pockets. The contents were placed on the desk. There was the money Papa had given him for swimming; a crumpled note Gary had passed him in class; a couple of elastic bands and paper clips; a ballpoint pen and his key. The key for which he had begged so hard. He watched them all dropped into a plastic bag. The final item to be taken was the watch Papa had given him for his last birthday. They were going to let him keep it until someone noticed a stain on the tan leather strap. The watch was carefully slipped into a separate bag. When he was presented with a long form, he simply signed wherever the finger pointed. A hand on his shoulder steered him into a cell and he slumped on to a wooden bench. There was nothing except the bench and a built-in toilet. He sat, dry-eyed, his mind incapable of taking in anything beyond the single thought: *James is alive.*

The moment Femi saw Papa, however, tears pricked at his eyes. With his grey-specked head slightly bowed, his father looked small next to the officer, who loomed more than a head above him. Papa's arms hung limply at his sides, one hand holding a plastic bag. His face revealed worry more than anger, making Femi want to throw himself into his father's arms. But an invisible barrier lay between them. He wanted to tell Papa that he didn't do it, but his mouth was dry. Instead, he ducked his head and gritted his teeth as he joined Papa in front of the charge desk.

This time, Femi made an effort to follow what was being said. Once again, the custody sergeant explained everything.

'What is the condition of the victim?' Papa asked.

'Critical.' The custody sergeant's eyes flicked from father to son.

Critical. Didn't that mean that James might still die?

Were doctors trying to save him? Femi wanted Papa to ask more questions, but he didn't.

'. . . I asked your son if he would like a legal adviser but –'

'I have a solicitor – Mr Nathan – let me ring him!' Femi thought he heard a quaver in Papa's voice. It had never trembled when Papa spoke to Mr Nathan about his asylum case.

'You can telephone him if you wish, sir, but it's late. I suggest you do it in the morning. The boy is exhausted. He needs to sleep. We shan't interview tonight.'

'Can I take him home?'

'Afraid not, sir. Bail is out of the question for a serious charge like this.'

'I'll bring him back first thing in the morning. I promise!' Femi had never heard Papa like this before. Pleading. His voice was rising unsteadily while the custody sergeant's tone remained calm, unchanged.

'Your son hasn't talked to us yet. He's our main suspect, sir.'

'Give me a chance to speak to him. He'll tell me the truth. He's not the kind of boy to do this kind of thing!'

'We are not going to interview until the morning, sir. As I said, it's a serious offence. If the victim dies, the charge could be murder.'

Murder. They thought he, Femi, could be a murderer! How could they get things so mixed up? Just because someone saw him running away . . . with a broken armrest they mistook for a gun! How could they think he would try to kill his big brother?

'. . . have you any reason to believe your son will try to harm himself, sir?'

Did they really think he had the energy to do

anything? He couldn't remember feeling so tired in all his life. All he wanted to do now was to sleep and never wake up.

'. . . we still need to do a strip search. We'd like you there, sir.'

A strip search. In front of Papa. He was too worn out even to be indignant.

Two policemen made him take off his clothes, one by one. Papa sat on the bench in the cell. Femi couldn't bear to look at him. Each item was carefully placed in a separate brown paper bag, including the bloodstained sweatshirt. An officer passed Femi the plastic bag that Papa had been carrying. He struggled to pull on his clean clothes.

'It's time to go, sir.' The officer was at the door. His colleague had already left with the brown bags. Femi stood in the middle of the cell with his head lowered.

'Femi?' Papa was willing him to look up. Willing him to say something.

'You can see your son in the morning, sir. We need to leave him to sleep.' It was clear who was in charge of him. The officer. Not Papa. Femi felt his father still hesitating.

'I'm coming, Officer. Just one minute – please.' Papa's voice sank to just above a whisper. Femi heard the note of desperation. 'Tell me, son – please – did you do this? However bad it is, we have to know the truth.'

If only he could release the words screaming inside him. *I didn't do it, Papa!* His head hung heavily and, although his lips parted, there was no sound. He needed to tell Papa, but instead he was shaking. Suddenly Papa's arms were around him, hugging him to his chest. For a brief moment, they held on to each other.

'I'll be back in the morning. *O da bo*, my son.'

Papa's arms slackened and he was gone. The door clanged shut and the key clattered in the lock. Femi lifted himself on to the bench and curled up. Never before had he felt so completely alone.

Sunday 12th October

2 a.m.

The phone rang after midnight and I thought it must be Papa so I jumped out of bed to pick it up before Mrs Wallace got it. It wasn't Papa. It was a low, rough voice:

'If that little brother talk foolish, you pay!'

Then the phone went dead. It sounded like Lizard Eyes! I was shaking so much I let Mrs Wallace put her arm around me. Next thing I knew, I was sitting on the sofa with her, telling her it was my fault that Femi had got in so deep with the wrong crowd. She tried to comfort me. She said I shouldn't put the blame all on to myself. The violence is much bigger. Gangs tell boys like Femi that they'll protect them. In Sierra Leone, some children join the rebels for the same reason. You mightn't believe this, Iyawo, but I cried on Mrs Wallace's shoulder. I couldn't help it. She made me hot chocolate and said I should go to sleep. I'm still trying to keep awake until Papa comes home but my eyelids feel like they are about to drop.

146

CHAPTER 27

No More Secrets

Femi woke to clanking, rattling, banging and heavy footsteps in the corridor outside. His cell door would be thrown open any minute. He pulled the sheet and blankets over his ears, trying to dull the sounds. His sleep had been punctured by bad dreams. The only thing he could remember clearly was a hand thrusting down with a knife. The hand was covered with a plastic glove. That confused him. He had seen Errol use a knife with his bare hand. Surgeons wore plastic gloves. Perhaps he had been dreaming about James having an operation. But a surgeon would use a knife carefully. Not stab it.

His mind ached. It almost felt as jumbled as his dreams. He was going to be interviewed this morning and Papa had said: 'We have to know the truth.' They would ask him what happened at the garage. Then they would want to know what happened before that ... and before that. How could he unravel everything? The stories in his head were a tangle of knots. The only clear thing was that each story linked him to Errol ... as if he were at one end and Errol was waiting for him at the other.

Unforgiving. That was how James had once described

Errol. If Errol were arrested, he would know that Femi had talked. If he couldn't get revenge himself, he had friends who could. How would James advise him now? Say nothing? Yet look how Errol had rewarded James for his loyalty! Whatever Femi said – nothing or everything – it was all hopeless.

Femi was still under his blankets with his head facing the wall when he heard a key in the lock. The door cranked open. He expected a police officer to shout at him to get up. Instead he heard Papa being let in.

'Femi?' Papa called softly.

Femi pretended not to stir. His father had hugged him last night, but by now he must have realized how much Femi had been lying to him. Papa hated liars.

'Worn out from last night. We can leave him another hour or so, sir. Detectives won't be in until eleven.'

He held his breath until he heard them turn to go. If he didn't speak quickly, Papa would leave him.

'I'm awake, Papa.' He rolled over slowly, keeping the blanket drawn up close to his face.

Without saying anything, Papa came to sit beside him. He placed his hand on Femi's shoulder. It was heavy and warm. The door banged and echoed. They were alone. It seemed an age before Papa spoke. He sounded more grave than severe.

'You can't keep hiding, Femi. There have to be no more secrets.'

Femi kept silent.

'I've spoken to Mr Nathan and he is prepared to come. But we can only help you if you tell us the truth.'

'They'll cut me up, Papa!' Femi whimpered.

'Who are these people?' Papa demanded.

Femi cringed. Papa would now be relentless.

'You have to tell the police everything, Femi. It's their job to deal with these criminals.'

'But Mama was killed because you told the truth, Papa!'

He hadn't meant to say that. It sounded like an accusation. He didn't know where the words had come from.

'Femi, the soldiers who govern our country at home are criminals! You are right. They killed Mama because they hated the truth that I wrote about them. But it wasn't the *truth* that killed her. It was those criminals!'

Papa's voice rumbled with fury and broke off suddenly. He took a deep breath.

'I should have been much more careful in protecting all of you. That was my fault. But it wasn't wrong to stand up to them, Femi. If you know something is wrong, you have to do something about it. Mama would have told you that too. Otherwise we let wrongdoers and bullies become dictators.'

Femi closed his eyes. Papa still stood by telling the truth. Whatever the consequences.

'Come on, Femi. Sit up now. We have to talk.'

Papa's hand was still resting on his shoulder. It was silently saying, *I'm not deserting you.* He had been expecting Papa's anger, not this. He wriggled himself up.

'Eh! That's better,' said Papa. 'Now tell me, how did this all begin?'

Where was the beginning? Femi bit his lip.

'Do you know the boy who was stabbed – this James Dalton?'

Femi's face burned. His mouth was dry again but he had to make himself speak.

'He was trying to protect me!' he whispered.

'Protect you from whom?' Papa asked bluntly.

Femi winced. His lips parted but he couldn't say Errol's name.

'All right, we'll come to that later. Let's start with James. Where did you first meet him? Remember, Femi, you need to tell me the *whole truth*.'

'He goes to my school. He – he –' Femi faltered, 'called me his little brother. He asked me to give Sade a message from someone.'

'Sade?' Femi could hear Papa's surprise. 'A message from whom?'

Femi swallowed.

'Errol. Errol Richards.' His voice was barely louder than a whisper.

'Why couldn't James give Sade the message himself?'

'I don't know.' It was true. He had never worked that out.

'Who is Errol Richards?'

'James's friend. He *was* James's friend until –' Femi bit his thumb hard. 'He's older than James.'

'Is he also in your school?'

Femi shook his head.

'He got expelled.' He could imagine Papa's face. He dared not look up.

With Papa's prodding, Femi began to piece together how he had got involved in the gang. How James had sent him a message to meet him at the Leisure Centre. How he had started hanging around with the gang on Saturdays.

'So you didn't go swimming?'

Femi shook his head.

'What about football?'

'No, Papa.' He hung his head.

'What did you do with the gang?'

The questions were coming faster. Surely Papa could hear his heart thumping?

'Did you steal?'

His head felt too heavy to nod, his eyes fixed to the cell floor. Papa began to ask about Errol. Piece by piece, Papa extracted each bit of information . . . about Errol waiting outside the school . . . at the old petrol station . . . the young men with him . . . everything except what had happened yesterday. Then Papa suddenly changed direction.

'You knew these boys were doing wrong. Why did you keep going with them?'

'You don't like me to go out, Papa,' he whispered. 'You always say something might happen. A gang is safer.'

'Safer?!' Papa expostulated. 'Aren't you leaving something out?'

This was the beginning of the explosion he had expected.

'Perhaps you are not telling yourself everything, Femi. Things you would rather forget.'

Papa had cut him open like a surgeon. He had been carefully probing, but now he was beginning to jab. Femi's lips began to quiver. Of course there were things he would rather forget. He felt sobs rising, shaking him. He clenched one hand around the other, trying to hold himself tight. He heard Papa breathe deeply and sigh.

'I just want to understand what was going on between the three of you.' Papa struggled to calm his voice, reining himself in. 'James and Errol offered to protect you. But did they ever threaten you?'

151

Femi hesitated. He dug his nails into his palms.

'Not James so much, Papa.' It was the nearest to the truth he could get without betraying James.

'Loyalty to friends is good, Femi, but it needs to be earned. Now, tell me what happened yesterday.'

There was no escape this time. He was being prepared for the detectives.

At first Femi kept to the bare details. James waiting for him outside the Leisure Centre. The quick march to the petrol station. The little packet and Errol's instructions for delivery. The men in the lift at Durrant Court. The brown envelope from the lady. The men waiting for him. The mugging in the lift. Running home . . .

'I was scared, Papa.' It was the first time he had said anything about how he had felt.

'Of whom?'

'Errol,' Femi whispered.

'And James?'

Femi wavered and bit his lip before giving a small nod.

'So you went to tell them?'

'I had to, Papa. They would have come for me.'

The images flashed through Femi's mind as he forced himself on. James's angry face. Errol grabbing him, twisting him with his hand behind his back, while James looked on. The knife grazing past his face. At last, James trying to stop Errol. A tangle of arms, bodies and blood. The armchair crashing beneath him. James telling him to run. His hand around the broken armrest. The sentries tearing through the door. One reaching for his pocket . . .

'They didn't see me, Papa. I got away – I was running

– but then I heard something like a shot. Like – like –'
He couldn't say it, but perhaps Papa guessed. *The shot that killed Mama.* Femi's voice broke down into sobs. Papa pulled him closer and let him weep.

CHAPTER 28

Scooped Out

Papa used to joke that Femi was like a tortoise hiding under his shell when he was silent. But now Femi felt as if he had been scooped out and there was nothing left inside. He hadn't eaten for twenty-four hours, but his stomach had been so cramped by fear that he hadn't noticed his hunger. Even after the cup of tea and two slices of toast, he felt empty. Drained.

Femi watched listlessly as Mr Nathan was ushered into his cell. Papa had told him how lucky he was that Mr Nathan had agreed to come, especially on a Sunday morning. Mr Nathan, with his wrinkled, weather-beaten face and blown-about grey hair, had helped Femi and Sade before. Femi remembered how Mr Nathan had tried to protect them from the immigration officers who insisted on taking their fingerprints as if they were criminals. Mr Nathan hadn't succeeded then. Perhaps he wouldn't be able to protect Femi from the detectives now.

Mr Nathan only had time to hear Femi say that he had never attacked James when a policewoman announced that the detectives were waiting.

'I advise you to tell them exactly what happened,' said Mr Nathan. 'Just tell them the truth.'

Femi wondered if Papa had asked him to say that.

'I shall sit through the interview and intervene if I think something is unfair. You don't have to answer their questions but – if you're not guilty – it's in your best interest to tell the police whatever you know.'

Best interest. Obviously Mr Nathan knew nothing about Errol.

It was a short way down a couple of corridors to the interview room. Walking in front with the policewoman, Femi heard Papa's anxious question to Mr Nathan.

'Will the police notify Immigration about this? Can it affect our application?'

Mr Nathan's reply was smothered by a sudden clamour. Someone was yelling and cursing while battering a door. Femi winced as if he were the object of the blows.

The first thing he noticed about the two detectives was that they were not in uniform. The second thing was that one detective was black, the first black officer he had seen at the police station. He was very tall, with broad square shoulders. Femi imagined the powerful muscles of someone who trained a lot. Not the kind of person to mess with. He was younger than the white officer, who had light grey hair, a narrow moustache and metal-rimmed glasses, similar to Papa's, over which he peered. Femi avoided both pairs of eyes but followed the large hands of the body-builder officer as he peeled the cellophane packaging off two tapes and inserted them into a recording machine.

Femi watched the tapes begin to turn as the older detective announced the date, the time and the names of everyone in the room. He explained what they were going to do. He made his voice sound ordinary. But Femi knew that the detectives were already prowling around him. They would examine his every word, as would Papa, who sat stiffly beside him, and Mr Nathan with his small wire-bound notebook. So would the fifth person in the room who stood invisibly at the door, circling him from behind dark shades. Only Femi knew he was there.

You think I stupid, Mister African bwoy!

But he had already told Papa the truth. There was no going back.

The questions seemed endless and he began to think that he had answered some of them before. They were setting him traps, weren't they? He was beginning to get muddled and his head was spinning when Mr Nathan interrupted.

'My client is getting tired. You've no evidence connecting him to the offence. He should be released.'

'That's not possible, sir. We've the blood all over his shirt! He was clearly a witness and we don't know yet that he's telling the truth,' the grey-moustached detective replied calmly.

'He's a vulnerable boy – a victim in all this – who got himself into something very nasty,' Mr Nathan persisted. 'You can tell he's scared out of his wits!'

'If you think we're going to let our only witness go before we've checked his story, you're sadly mistaken, sir. This could still turn into a murder inquiry.'

Femi's heart froze.

'We'll bring in Errol Richards,' the body-builder added quietly. 'Once we've interviewed him, we'll decide about Femi.'

He had told them the truth, but they were still going to keep him! He was exhausted and it took too much energy to follow what Mr Nathan was saying. Wearily, he watched the tapes being individually sealed and one handed to his father. What was Papa meant to do with it? Listen to it over and over again? When he saw a black-and-white uniform at the door, he got up without being asked. He just wanted to get back to the cell, to sleep, to forget. As he left the room, he heard Papa say in a hushed voice that he would like a word with the detectives. Something about a threatening phone call. Papa didn't need to whisper. Femi didn't want to hear.

Sunday 12th October

6 p.m.

Femi's story is coming out. I know hate is wrong but that's what I feel for Lizard Eyes, even if it's wrong. He NEARLY KILLED Femi. Only James Dalton stopped him and got stabbed instead. Papa says Lizard Eyes sent Femi to do his dirty work, delivering his drugs, and then went mad when Femi was beaten up and the money was stolen. Now I know why Femi was in such a state when he came home yesterday. Everything is beginning to fit. But the police still won't let him go. They say they can't know if he's telling the truth until they've interviewed Lizard Eyes. But he's not going to tell them the truth, is he? The only person who might is James and he's

156

still in a critical condition. What if he dies? I feel numb thinking about him lying there — and knowing it could have been Femi.

Aunt Gracie and Uncle Roy have been here all afternoon. Papa has told them everything. They are sure the police will release Femi and they insist we go and stay with them so the gang won't know where he is. Aunt Gracie kept going on about little Bonzo and Marco next door. In the end Papa told me to pack my bag and one for Femi as well. I'm amazed that Papa hasn't exploded yet. I think we are all still spinning. The fireworks are still to come.

I can't help thinking of when we had to leave Nigeria. I remember looking at my bedroom and wondering when I'd ever see it with all my precious things again. Like you, Iyawo. I was so happy when Papa brought you to me. Anyway, this is different and I don't want to keep moving you and Oko. It's unsettling. I've only packed for a few days. Mr Nathan is pressing for Femi to be freed and we are just waiting for a phone call from the police.

P.S. Mrs Wallace has gone back to her own place even though Papa didn't look happy about it.

11 p.m. (Aunt Gracie's. My old room)

Femi is back and, at last, the police are questioning Lizard Eyes! I've never seen my little brother look so shamefaced. His head hung down like a puppet's without a string. Aunt Gracie wanted him to eat some supper but he didn't want anything. He's gone to sleep in his old room and I'm next door. I'm writing at the table underneath the window with the yellow-and-green pineapple curtains. Papa is sleeping on the sofa bed in the living room, just like he did when he was released from the Detention Centre two years ago. We celebrated when Papa came out but no one celebrated tonight. Aunt Gracie and Uncle Roy are very kind but it feels strange to be back here. Like we're going backwards.

CHAPTER 29

Rumours

Sade tried to take no notice of the glances as Papa walked with her into Avon High School on Monday morning. They had left Femi sleeping at Aunt Gracie's. Papa was coming to speak to Flash Gordon so the school would know the truth rather than relying on rumours. Papa also said he wanted to find out more about James and his gang. She kept the thought to herself that Papa was wasting his time. What did Flash Gordon or any of the teachers know about what went on outside lessons?

She left her father waiting at the school office and headed straight for her tutor group. Mariam greeted her in the corridor beside their tutor room.

'What's this about James Dalton?' asked Mariam, adjusting the headphones under her scarf. 'They say he was stabbed and your brother was there!'

'I know,' Sade mumbled. Her heart sank. Rumours were already flying. Even before entering the class-room, she sensed that people were talking about James. The desk where he usually sat in the far corner was empty and a group of students were clustered around Marcia. Voices were rising. Marcia's was the loudest, but it stopped as soon as Sade appeared at the door.

Marcia scowled. Sade would have ignored her but Marcia threw out a challenge.

'You've got a nerve, showing your face!'

Sade stared back. Marcia trampled over anyone who showed weakness.

'What do you mean?' Sade asked steadily.

'Don't play innocent. Your brother is a lying little git. He's got my brother in trouble. The police came crawling all over our house!'

'Aren't you leaving something out?' Sade was surprised at how calmly her voice hovered in the air above the sudden quiet.

'What?' Marcia thrust her chin forward. Today her hair was in plaits, bunched together in a swinging ponytail, with clicking beads.

'That's for your brother to tell the police,' Sade replied sharply. 'If he and James want to kill each other, that's nothing to do with Femi.'

'My brother never had beef with James until you came along, Miss Queen of Africa.'

Marcia was spoiling for a fight! Imagine accusing her, Sade, of coming between James and Lizard Eyes! Her stomach tightened and her heart beat faster, but she shrugged her shoulders as if she couldn't be bothered to reply.

Mariam pressed closer. 'What's your problem, Marcia?' Mariam demanded. 'Sade's never –'

'What's going on here? Quieten down, Year Ten!' Sade caught her breath as Mr Morris's voice cut in from behind. She and Mariam moved aside to let their form tutor into the room.

'I have serious news about a member of our form,' he said severely.

159

Marcia glowered, before turning her back. She flounced to her desk with Donna in tow. As Sade and Mariam slipped into their seats on the other side of the room, it struck Sade that Donna had been unusually quiet.

As he called out names for registration, Mr Morris lowered his voice at 'James Dalton' but didn't stop. Instead of the usual chatter, the class was hushed and tense, waiting for the announcement.

'I expect most of you already know that James was stabbed on Saturday.' Mr Morris surveyed the class. 'I'm glad to say we've just heard that the doctors have taken him off the critical list.'

Sade closed her eyes, letting the cheers ripple past her. Of course it was good news. Since the moment she had heard that James was fighting for his life, she had largely thought about what it would mean to Femi if James told the truth. She had tried not to think too much about James ... the boy with a quick mind and tongue who used to make her laugh in Reading Club ... the boy who used to have more sense about him than most of the others his age ... the boy who had won the Maths Prize in Year Eight ... whose proud mother had asked Sade to take a photo of them with James beaming as he held his certificate and prize book ... the boy who had changed. The police would interview him as soon as he was well enough. But would he tell them the truth? Or would he continue to be loyal to the person who had nearly killed him?

Monday 13th October

9 p.m.

I'm too emotional and mixed up to write much tonight. James is out of danger and we are waiting for the police to question him. Marcia tried to pick a fight with me — as if I'm responsible for her maniac brother getting arrested! I tried not to get drawn in. Why hang up your dirty clothes for everyone to see? But to tell you the truth, Iyawo, I'm not just fed up with myself for all the reasons you know. I'm still very angry at Femi. Aunt Gracie says he stayed in his bedroom all day and hardly ate a thing. She says he is still in shock. So what about the rest of us? If I write what I really feel right now — and the mess we are in because of Femi — later I'll probably be ashamed of what I write. It's best to shut up.

Tuesday 14th October

8 p.m.

Unbelievable. THE POLICE HAVE LET LIZARD EYES GO. He was back outside school this afternoon, in his usual pose underneath the silver coupé. Face like a mask behind the dark glasses. Lots of people around him and Marcia crowing like he's a hero. It turned me to jelly inside. Papa went to see the police. They said that the doctors had let them interview James this morning. He told them it was Lizard Eyes who stabbed him, but it was AN ACCIDENT! He says Femi misunderstood. The police say the case against Lizard Eyes is now too weak. The drugs thing is another matter and, anyway, they didn't find any on him. So they had to let him go! There I was, thinking that at least James had the courage to save Femi. How stupid of me to dream for a minute that he might have the courage to go against Lizard Eyes. It's sickening. A near murderer is going free and I can hear his voice: 'If that little brother talk foolish, you pay.'

CHAPTER 30

Hard Choices

In the days following his release, Femi was easily tearful. When Papa began a 'serious talk', Femi sat still and motionless except for his tears. They seemed to come from a source over which he had no control. Papa abandoned the talk. Most unusually, Papa also let him stay away from school. Femi felt drained of energy and didn't get up until long after Papa and Sade had left the house. Aunt Gracie tried to coax him with food, including his favourite fried plantains, but when she tried to get him to talk he clammed up. For much of the time she left him watching television or reading old comics. When Papa came back for supper, before going out again to do his night shift at the cab office, he didn't pressure Femi to speak. Sade left him alone as well. Although she said nothing, he sensed that his sister was angry with him.

One evening, Uncle Roy set up a game of chess and called Femi to play. Uncle Roy had taught him over a year ago but now he found it an effort to concentrate and lost three pawns in a row.

'It's like in life, you know,' Uncle Roy said. 'The small pawns are the first to be thrown away.'

Femi suspected that Uncle Roy was trying to make a

point about him. Had he let himself be a pawn? He soon lost interest in the game.

However, it was impossible to keep his mind blank. A lot of the time he stayed in his room, lying on the bed, trying to make sense of the muddle in his head. He had been encouraged to tell the truth to the police. Then they had let Errol go! It was as if the jigsaw in his head had been thrown into the air. According to James, it was all a misunderstanding. Errol had drawn out the knife only to scare them but hadn't meant to use it. Things had just gone wrong.

Was it possible that he had misunderstood? Hadn't he seen Errol flare up before and then act as if nothing had ever happened? Despite everything, James and Errol were still brethren. If, like James, Femi had simply said that the stabbing was an accident, what could the police have done? Instead, he had told the police everything. All about the delivery of the packet, how he had gone to Durrant Court and what happened there. Everything. Errol would never forgive him for his betrayal. Nor would James. Even Papa had taken the threat seriously enough to move them out of their flat.

On Saturday morning, Femi woke to the sound of water running in the bathroom. He pulled his duvet over his head. Soon everyone in the house would be up except him. Aunt Gracie would probably come to ask if she could make him something for breakfast. But if he went downstairs, he would find Papa waiting for him. The night before, Papa had told him that they couldn't delay any more. Decisions had to be made. They couldn't stay with Aunt Gracie and Uncle Roy

163

forever and he wouldn't be allowed to stay away from school any longer. There had to be – as Papa called it – a 'family conference'.

It was Papa who called him to breakfast. Afterwards, when Femi tried to slip away from the table, Papa steered him back with his outstretched hand.

'Stay here, son! You can't keep running away. It's time to talk.'

Femi flopped back down on the chair next to Sade. He avoided looking at anyone by keeping his eyes fixed on the marmalade.

'If our situation was different, I would send you straight back to Nigeria. Put you in boarding school there. I've discussed it with your Uncle Tunde many times, but it's still too risky.'

This was going to be a lecture, not a talk. Papa lowered his voice.

'What happened to Mami Cynthie's boy reminds us how lawless people stop at nothing.'

Lawless people stop at nothing. But they weren't just in Africa, were they?

'I've been to the Housing Office,' Papa continued. 'They've put us on the list to move to another area, but we have to wait.'

'What about my school, Papa?' Sade protested. 'I don't want to move in the middle of my exam course!'

'I'm just exploring our choices, Sade. Hard choices. I've been wondering if we should join your Uncle Dele in Devon.'

Both children were silent. They had visited Uncle Dele in the summer holidays. They had enjoyed the beach and the sea, and most people in his village had been friendly. But when they had gone into the town, Femi recalled some stares and awkward glances.

'The problem is that until we can get proper refugee status, it's much better for us to be in London. At least I have work here that brings us some money.'

Refugee status. There it was again. The immigration officers held a giant cloud over them, threatening a storm at any time. Papa was talking about choices but it seemed they didn't have any.

'But I could send *you* to your uncle, Femi –'

'I don't want to go without you, Papa!' he cried.

'Marco's parents sent him away, after Bonzo was shot,' Sade reminded him curtly. 'At least Lizard Eyes and his gang won't find you there.'

Femi felt his eyes beginning to prick.

'Our only other choice –' Papa hesitated, 'is for the three of us to go back to our flat. Sade can stay at Avon but I shall have to move you to another school – away from those bad boys.'

Go back to our flat ... move you to another school. Elephants with giant butterfly ears were stampeding through him again. Even if he went to another school, Errol would find him! Waylay him on the way home. Tears blurred the marmalade jar and everything else on the table.

'Errol will still get me, Papa! If I had the money I could give it to him, then he would leave me alone!' Femi whimpered.

'Even if we had the money, my boy, we couldn't do that. What Errol and his friends were doing was illegal. Besides, when you give in to bullies, they bully you more.'

He wanted to shut out Papa's words, stop them

whirling around inside his head. They just made him feel worse.

'When you start a fire, Femi, it has flames,' Papa went on quietly. 'If I send you to a new school, I shall have to take and collect you.'

So he was going to be under constant supervision! This was his choice. Being sent away or living like a prisoner. The police might as well have kept him locked up! Suddenly his arms were flailing as he pushed his chair away from the table. It clattered to the floor behind him. He didn't stop to pick it up. Through his tears he caught a glimpse of Papa's startled face and dived for the dining-room door. He flung himself past Aunt Gracie, who had come to see what was happening, and dashed towards the stairs. This time Papa didn't even try to stop him.

CHAPTER 31

Memories

The rage that had stormed through Femi left him exhausted. He wanted to go back to sleep and forget what had just happened, but his whole body felt uncomfortable. He had behaved terribly. In Nigeria, most of his school friends had fathers who beat them whenever they stepped out of line. Femi had been the only one whose father had never hit him. Some of his friends had mothers who complained about them to their fathers. But if Mama ever had a problem with Femi, she used to talk to him herself. Only once, in England, Papa had come near to beating him. But after he had undone his belt, Femi had seen that his father's hand was shaking. Papa had threaded the belt back and Femi still hadn't forgotten what he had said: 'Your Mama's spirit won't let me do it. If I beat you, I have lost the argument.'

If his friends had got into this kind of trouble, their fathers would have beaten them until the children were begging for mercy. There would have been no 'family conference'. But, instead of thinking he was lucky to have a father who wanted to talk with him, he had lost his temper. Flown into a wild frenzy. When he had kicked his chair, it was like he had kicked Papa.

Femi turned away from his wall to face his chest of drawers. His eyes travelled up to the top of the chest and the family photograph in a slim dark-green frame. He had found it among the clothes in his bag. Sade must have put it there. He had become so used to it being on his shelf in his bedroom in their flat that he hadn't looked at it for a long time. He stretched out for it now, then curled back again on to his bed, the photo propped against his pillow. There were Mama and Papa in front of the flaming forest tree in their yard at home, with Sade and himself in front. He had been nine at the time, standing tall and grinning. Mama's left arm held him close while Papa's hands rested on Sade's shoulders. His sister looked proud and pleased. Mama had her gentle smile while Papa seemed to be caught in the middle of saying something. Femi stared miserably at the four of them. Why couldn't they have stayed liked that? Just a happy family?

Everything had been so different in Lagos. Another world in which he played football every day between the flaming forest and the pawpaw trees in their own compound. The sun was always bright, except when the harmattan wind threw a dusty haze over everything. He missed the heat on his skin and then being drenched when the whole sky became the most powerful waterfall in the world. He missed all his friends, cousins, aunties, uncles and, perhaps more than anything, the journeys to see Grandma at Family House.

Grandma had always made a special prayer after their long journey along the highway and the pot-holed roads through the bush. Everyone in the village knew them. When they arrived, they couldn't walk anywhere without stopping a hundred times to exchange greetings and news! There would be nights of stories with Baba Akin, whose face was even more wrinkled than Mr Nathan's. He could mysteriously change his voice from a rabbit to a lion, a young girl to a crocodile, a boy to an old woman. All the while, the smoke from his pipe would weave past his leathery face to disappear into the darkness above. If Femi was ever reminded of one of his stories, he also smelt the sharpness of Baba Akin's tobacco.

In the daytime at Family House there would be games of chasing goats and chickens until the bleating and squawking brought an adult to tell them off. There was also Baba Baobab to climb – the oldest tree in the world! Every Christmas the children stretched their hands around its trunk and argued about how much it had grown. Grandma would say: 'That old tree will outlive me. It will still be here when you are a grown man.'

Ever since he had come to England, it upset Femi to remember back home. What was the point in thinking about it when you couldn't go there? But today he was so wretched, he didn't even try to stop the memories that came from before the final, fatal day that he never wanted to remember. He found them strangely calming. They reminded him of a time when he had just been himself and everything had its right place.

When he woke, the room was in darkness. He switched on the bedside light and looked at his watch. Almost six o'clock. The house felt very quiet, not even the faint sound of television. No one had called him for dinner, not even Aunt Gracie. He was not surprised. Shame came flooding back to him. He would have continued lying there, ignoring the ache in his stomach, but he knew it was up to him to go and apologize. He had to tell Papa that he would go to Uncle Dele. He didn't want to go away, but living in fear of Errol every day would be worse.

The only light downstairs came from the kitchen. Femi found Aunt Gracie sitting at the table, reading the newspaper. She looked up, deliberately waiting for him to speak first.

'Auntie, where is Papa?'

Aunt Gracie folded the newspaper.

'Your papa has gone with Sade and Uncle Roy to check the flat.'

There was an awkward silence as Femi's mind fumbled over what to say.

'I – I'm sorry I lost my temper, Auntie.'

'It's your father who needs to hear it, Femi.'

'I know, Auntie,' he whispered. 'I'll tell him when he comes.'

'They may be quite late, you know. They were going to call on Mrs Wallace as well.'

Femi felt an ache in his stomach. He was hungry but too embarrassed to say so. He turned to go back upstairs but Aunt Gracie called him back.

'Do you want something to eat, Femi?'

He nodded quickly.

'Yes, please, Auntie.'

'Well, come and sit down here while I heat something. My mother used to say that feeling hungry is a good sign.'

He could tell that Aunt Gracie was not going to let him slip away to watch television. She wanted him to talk. After everything that had happened, he could no longer remain stubbornly silent. But Aunt Gracie didn't ask questions like a detective. Instead, she began by recounting a tale of a playground bully when she was a child and how her older brother had ambushed him one day to teach him a lesson. Little by little, she provoked him into talking. Femi could feel her winkling him out as she asked questions about his friends at school ... first Gary, the children in his class, then, after a while, James. Femi wondered how much Papa had told her and Uncle Roy. She was a sympathetic listener, but he was glad when, after he had eaten, she let him go to the television.

He kept wondering when Papa would return. The later it got, the more uncertain he began to feel again about how to face his father. He was losing energy

170

again and by ten o'clock he could hardly keep his eyes open.

'You can talk to your papa in the morning,' Aunt Gracie said. 'I'll tell him you wanted to wait up for him, but I sent you up.'

Femi hurried upstairs. His apology – and everything else – could wait until the morning. He fell asleep almost as soon as his head hit the pillow.

A cry from his sister and urgent voices outside his bedroom brought him tumbling out of bed early in the morning. By the time he reached the landing, still half asleep, Aunt Gracie, Uncle Roy and Sade were clustered around Papa at the bottom of the stairs. To his horror, Femi made out two police officers standing in the hallway. They hadn't come for him again, had they? Or had they come for Papa? Had the immigration people sent for him? Then he heard the word. *Fire!* Suddenly he understood. Their flat had been set alight in the middle of the night! He heard Papa tell the police that he had been there only a few hours ago. Everything in the flat had been fine last night. No, he had left nothing on that could have started a fire.

From the top step, Femi watched numbly as Papa pulled on his coat and Sade insisted that she was going with him. As she scurried up the stairs to change out of her nightclothes, she passed Femi as if he were invisible. Aunt Gracie bustled back and forth in the hallway, searching for Uncle Roy's shoes. He was going to drive Papa and Sade. Papa opened the front door, letting in an icy blast. He tramped out behind the two police officers, without looking back. Femi wanted to cry out,

'I'm sorry!' but the words froze in his head. He knew who was responsible.

CHAPTER 32

Ashes

'If we had been inside – sleeping – we couldn't have got out!' Sade heard the catch in Papa's voice. She hovered beside him by the gaping hole that had been their front door, staring into the blackened shell that had been their living room. It was littered with strange, skeletal shapes and looked like a bombsite doused by a thunderstorm. The mixture of burnt smells was almost overpowering.

A few hours ago, it must have been a raging inferno. At six o'clock in the morning it was eerily quiet. The neighbours who had been evacuated had been allowed back home, including Mrs Beattie. The police said she had been woken by an explosion shortly after midnight and called 999 immediately. If she hadn't been so prompt, the damage would have been much worse . . . perhaps even lives lost.

The police told them not to disturb things inside the flat. They still had to investigate. It was likely that petrol had been poured through the letterbox and set alight. It appeared that the fire had raged through the living room and kitchen first, before spreading down the passage to the bedrooms. Whatever wasn't burnt was smeared with thick layers of ash. The pools of water on the floor looked like oil slicks. They stared in shocked silence. But when Papa saw the remains of his computer, he groaned. All the papers and files that had been stacked up alongside it were a pile of cinders.

Sade picked her way along the blackened corridor until she reached her bedroom. She steadied herself against the doorframe. She could have been peering at the dark negative of a photograph. Her stomach swirled, something bitter rising up through her throat. She swallowed. Was this her room? Then she saw her Iyawo and Oko. Sitting on the charred remains of her desk, they looked like ancient figures petrified and preserved by volcanic lava. Relics from another age. The flames must have been licking around them, scorching away the silk-smooth ebony, when the fire fighters arrived to do battle here in her bedroom.

Forgetting what she had been told, Sade stepped across the floor. There was something that couldn't wait. She tugged the handle of the lowest desk drawer. It crumbled under her touch. She used her finger-nails to prise open the drawer and cried out. The fire had attacked the desk from underneath. Her precious Iyawo book – her first one – had been tucked safely away in the bottom drawer. Now it lay in the melted, charred debris below the desk. It could have been the remains of a slice of burnt toast. She bent down and touched it gingerly, her fingers sinking into ash. Her mouth was dry, her head pounding. All those words she had written were lost forever. All those thoughts, memories and feelings that she had once confided to her first Iyawo book were wiped out. This was the one book in her room that could never be replaced. It had been the only copy in the world. Oh why hadn't she taken it to Aunt Gracie's? How stupid not to have realized that something like this could happen! It was the reason why Aunt Gracie had insisted they leave the flat in the first place.

Ignoring the instruction not to move anything, Sade gently lifted the Iyawo head, then Oko. They still felt warm. Not caring about the soot covering her hands and clothes, she retreated, cradling them in her arms. However damaged and disfigured, she was not going to leave them here.

Sade found Mrs Beattie with Papa. She was in her dressing gown and was gripping Papa by the wrist.

'Honest to God, I thought I was back in Belfast with the Troubles. The explosion rocked me clean out of bed!' Mrs Beattie's hand was shaking like her voice.

'Thank you very much for calling the police, Mrs Beattie.' Papa placed his free hand over hers, trying to steady her. 'If you hadn't been so prompt, it could have been much worse.'

'By the time I got to the door, they'd fled, the cowards! But I looked over the balcony. I saw one running! A black jacket, he had, with something like silver flashing down the arm. They could have set us all on fire. I hope the police get 'em and throw away the key!'

'Lizard Eyes – I mean Errol – has a jacket like that, Papa!' Sade exclaimed.

Before Papa could reply, the two policemen re-emerged from the outside corridor. One of them gently but firmly prised Mrs Beattie away from Papa.

'Come, Mrs Beattie. Best for you to rest now. We'll be

along later to take a statement. You don't want to tire yourself out.'

The second officer turned to Papa.

'Will you come to the station with us, sir? We need a statement from you right away.'

Papa's face was almost as ashen as his hair, and his arms hung limply by his sides. He suddenly looked older.

'You go back with Uncle Roy, Sade.' Papa's gaze lingered for a moment on Iyawo and Oko in her arms. Sade dropped her head to battle silently with her tears.

Back at the Kings' house, she wiped Oko and Iyawo tenderly with sheets of wet kitchen paper. Their noses, ears and lips as well as Iyawo's plaits were all badly bitten by fire. Their smooth, shiny, ebony cheeks were dried out, rough, pock-marked. But the distinctive shape of each head was still there.

'What are you doing?' Femi asked plaintively.

Sade didn't answer as she carried Oko and Iyawo up the stairs, into her bedroom.

'Please, Sade. Talk to me! Please.' Femi followed her but stopped at the open doorway.

Sade placed Iyawo and Oko carefully on her desk. Then, pulling some clean clothes from the cupboard, she pushed past Femi and escaped to the bathroom.

CHAPTER 33

The Smell of Revenge

At first Femi did not recognize the two charred lumps of wood in Sade's arms. But when she placed them by the kitchen sink, as carefully as if they were delicate china, he realized that they were the ebony heads she always kept on her desk. He watched her wipe them as if she were a nurse cleaning her patients' wounds. Her face was smudged and tear-stained. When he tried to talk to her, she dismissed him roughly. She probably believed that this was also his fault.

Femi listened to Uncle Roy describe the burnt-out flat. Aunt Gracie kept shaking her head in disbelief. It was impossible for Femi to imagine everything completely destroyed. What had happened to his room and all his possessions? He had to see for himself. It would only take twenty minutes to walk there. But what if he bumped into Errol or someone from the gang? It was probably too early for any of them to be out in the streets on a Sunday morning, but he couldn't be sure. Papa was in the police station, right at this moment, telling the police that Errol was the prime suspect. If the police pulled him in for questioning but couldn't find any evidence, they would have to let him go again. He would want more revenge. He and his friends would trace the family to Aunt Gracie's house. What was to stop them coming to this quiet street? Where would it all end? Femi was caught in a maze from which there was no exit.

He paced the bedroom, hitting his fist into his palm. If he couldn't go out, he might as well be a prisoner. He had spent the greater part of the last week in this room, most of the time in bed. Aunt Gracie said he was recovering, but he actually felt worse. He had done nothing except get more muddled with the thoughts in his head. Instead of enjoying a week off school, he had missed the activity, chat, commotion, people. Most of all, he had missed Gary. Remembering how offhand he had been recently with his classmate, Femi felt ashamed. Hadn't he been cutting Gary out and leaving him on his own whenever it suited him? There must have been all kinds of rumours in school about his arrest. Yet he hadn't even bothered to ring Gary after he was released. What kind of friend was he? If Gary had decided that he was better off without him, he wouldn't be surprised.

The more Femi thought about Gary, the more desperately he wanted to talk to him. It might help clear up some of the muddle in his head. Gary was the most even-tempered person he knew. He had never known him to get mad at anyone or anything. Perhaps he had pushed Gary too far – but how would he know until he tried to talk with him? Femi suddenly knew what he had to do.

When Gary came to the telephone, he sounded half asleep until he realized it was Femi. He jerked awake.

'Where've you been? Is it true you nearly got done for murder? I've rung every night, but no one ever answers.'

Femi swallowed. Gary wasn't mad at him.

'I'm at my auntie's.'

It wasn't far from where Gary lived.

'You should see my new computer game! Come over. I'll call for you.' Gary put the phone down before Femi could say that he would need to get permission.

Immediately Femi replaced the receiver, an idea seeded itself. If he was allowed to go out with Gary, by making a short diversion on the way to his house they could see the burnt-out flat. They could use the main road and avoid the garage. The gang wouldn't be around so early on a Sunday morning. But if they did meet anyone, this time he was not going to be parted from his friend. Gary knew about steering clear of trouble. As long as he stuck with Gary, he'd be OK.

Femi willed Gary to come before Papa returned so he would only have to ask Aunt Gracie. She probably wouldn't grill Gary as closely as Papa. Only last night he had been telling her about Gary and she had said, 'He sounds like a nice friend.' However, when Gary arrived, Aunt Gracie was reluctant to let Femi go.

'Why don't you two boys play here until your papa comes, Femi?' It was a statement rather than a real question.

'But I need fresh air and exercise, Auntie! I've stayed inside too long!' Femi tried to control the whine in his voice.

'Well, the two of you can play football out at the back.'

Femi was tempted to say something about Gary not being able to stay for long, but he held back. He didn't want to start lying to Aunt Gracie. It was Uncle Roy who came to the rescue. He asked Gary where he lived.

'Femi's friend doesn't stay far, Gracie. Let them go together. We can't keep the child wrapped up forever, you know.'

Aunt Gracie's forehead puckered in doubt. Femi's eyes begged her to agree.

'All right,' she said finally. 'But I want you back here by one o'clock sharp for your dinner. Is that clear?'

Femi felt a surge of energy.

'Yes, Auntie.' He nodded vigorously. 'Thank you, Uncle Roy.' Femi grabbed his anorak from the coat-stand.

'What's going on?' Gary had been very quiet inside the house. His question burst like a small charge as soon as they had closed the door.

Femi scrunched up his face. 'Trouble, man. Trouble. Tons of it! We could all have been dead!'

'How?' Gary looked bemused.

'Errol tried to kill us! I swear it must have been him. Petrol. Matches. Kerwhoosh! If we'd been sleeping in our flat, we'd have been trapped, man!'

Femi tugged Gary's arm and pulled him past Uncle Roy's red roses to the gate.

'We've got to inspect the damage. Race you to the estate, right!'

Femi broke into a sprint before Gary could ask anything else.

'I'll tell you everything when we get there!' Femi called, leaving Gary no choice but to follow.

The morning mist was fresh and thick. Femi was glad. It made them less visible. Gary jogged alongside him at a steady pace. But even by the end of the road, Femi could feel himself lagging. One week of no exercise and already he was unfit. By the time they crossed over the High Street, he was short of breath and struggling to keep up. Gary slowed down until they were both walking. Femi knew his friend was waiting for him to talk. There was no point putting it off any longer.

'You know James – how he acted – like he was my older brother –' Femi struggled for the words.

'Yeah. He blanked me!' Gary said with a hint of disapproval.

Femi sighed. This was not going to be easy. He couldn't just start with the events of last Saturday. He had to explain how things had built up: from James taking him to meet Errol to delivering Errol's messages; from meeting the gang to 'doing stuff' with them; how one thing had led to another. He began slowly and stiffly, but then his voice revved up to roll over some details as swiftly as possible. When he came to the mugging and Errol's attack, however, he described them almost blow by blow. Gary was aghast. Why had the police let Errol go?

'James won't be negative to Errol 'cause he's like his brother, right! He said it was an accident. Errol didn't mean it.' Femi dug his hands into the pockets of his jacket. 'But my dad said to tell the truth. That's why Errol wants to kill me and my family. You get it?'

Gary sucked the air between his teeth.

'Errol is scary, man!'

They had entered the estate and fell silent as they

approached Femi's block. It was still too misty to see clearly up to the flat from the tarmac below. Femi led the way, bounding up the stairs two at a time. Their footsteps clattered against the concrete. There were puddles of water in the stairwells. Only a few hours ago, fire officers had been pounding up here. Femi's chest tightened as he scrambled on to the second-floor corridor. His hand shot up to his nose and mouth, but there was no escaping the smell. The ceiling and walls were blackened. The fire had licked its way almost to Mrs Beattie's door. He skidded to a stop, with Gary behind him. Someone had nailed wooden boards over the doorway and window of their flat and completely shut it up! There wasn't even a single chink through which he could peep into his own home. Sade had rescued her Iyawo and Oko, but he had nothing except this burnt stench in his nostrils and throat. Imagine if they had been inside! What would James have to say about this? Collecting petrol, carrying, pouring and lighting it could never be described as 'an accident'. This time there could be no misunderstanding. No doubt what Errol had meant.

Femi slid to the floor, his back against the balcony. He dropped his head between his knees, covering it with his hands. Gary's voice seemed to come from far away, asking if he was OK. Then another voice joined him.

'A terrible shock, to be sure. Will we bring him inside?' Mrs Beattie was hovering over him.

'I've got to get him home.'

Gary was closer now, on the floor beside him. Home? What home was he talking about?

'Let's get out of here, Femi.' His friend was pleading.

He felt a hand under his armpit, stretching around his waist.

'Lean on me.' Gary wanted to lever him up.

'He could do with a strong cup of tea. I'll put the kettle on.' Mrs Beattie's bird-like tutting noises faded as her footsteps shuffled away.

'We can't stay. here, Femi. Errol might send somebody!' Gary's voice was now desperate. It was the mention of Errol, however, that finally jolted him. He felt Gary's arm help lift him. It steered him along the corridor and he didn't resist. It stopped him from toppling over as they catapulted down the stairs. The mist that had shrouded them on their way to the flat was rising rapidly. They could be seen clearly from a distance now. Gary's arm, slung across his shoulder, slowed their pace but was reassuring. It reminded Femi that he wasn't utterly alone.

CHAPTER 34

Arm in Arm

Sunday 19th October

10 a.m.

Sade's Iyawo book lay open on the desk in front of her, her pen idle in the crease. She had written the time ten minutes ago, but the rest of the page lay blank. She sat staring out of the bedroom window. Instead of the russet-red and golden-brown leaves, she imagined flames engulfing the terrace of houses beyond the back gardens. Attacking the bricks, crackling around windows, exploding panes, forcing entry under billowing black clouds. With flames in pursuit from the back, would the people inside be able to escape through their front doors? The flames would consume everything. Like her anger. She understood her anger against Lizard Eyes – and also James. But her anger at Femi frightened her. It was no longer rational, she knew. He had been taught a terrible lesson, so what was the point in going on at him? Yet she was almost as furious with herself! None of this would have happened if she had been the responsible older sister. She had felt aggrieved when Papa had said he was disappointed in her. She had told herself that Papa didn't appreciate how much she still thought and acted like at home in Nigeria. But it wasn't actually true. If it was, she would have spoken to Papa as soon as she suspected her brother was getting into trouble. In Nigeria, it would have been expected of her. Her natural duty. Everything had been so much clearer at home. But here, in England, she no longer knew how to behave.

Sade heard the doorbell. She strained to hear if it was Papa returning from the police station. It wasn't. Instead, she heard Mrs Wallace asking Aunt Gracie anxiously about the fire. Papa must have rung her. Had she perhaps lost something in the fire? Some papers, maybe, or books? Then Sade remembered. Losing a few possessions would be nothing compared with losing a child. She shut her eyes. Mrs Wallace hadn't been to see them all week. Edward was still missing, according to Papa.

Sade remained in the bedroom with the blank page in front of her. But when Aunt Gracie came upstairs and asked Sade to take Mrs Wallace to the grocer's shop, she didn't protest. Mrs Wallace had offered to show Aunt Gracie how she made her special pepper soup, and they needed red peppers.

As soon as they had shut the gate, it was clear that Mrs Wallace wanted to talk to Sade. She was direct.

'It's a miracle that no one is dead. We have to look on the positive side, Sade.'

Sade was quiet. The morning fog hadn't yet lifted and she concentrated on the pavement ahead. There was hardly much to be positive about.

'I hope you are not blaming yourself.' Mrs Wallace unexpectedly linked her arm with Sade's. 'Blaming yourself won't help, you know. I talk from experience.'

Their eyes met briefly. Mrs Wallace's were as sharp as radar.

'I know how easy it is to destroy oneself with guilt. Of course we should admit when we have made mistakes. But we can take it too far. We all need friends to stop us doing that.'

She wasn't talking down to her as a child. She was speaking about herself. Sade had actually heard Papa telling her, 'You can't keep blaming yourself, Cynthie. It stops you thinking straight.' Sade didn't know what to say. They were walking in step at a steady pace.

'Is Papa very angry with me?' The question came out without planning. 'I think he's trying not to show it. But I need to know the truth.'

'Your papa is like everyone else, Sade. He wouldn't

be human if he hadn't been angry,' she said gently. 'I think he was upset – more than angry – that you didn't tell him any of your worries about Femi. But he blames himself as much as anyone. He wishes he had spent more evenings at home – that he hadn't put so much responsibility on your shoulders.'

'He had to get us money to live, didn't he? He couldn't help it.'

'That's just what I said to him, Sade. Perhaps no one could have stopped Femi joining that gang. Boys don't feel safe on these streets. They think that if they join a gang they'll be safer.' Mrs Wallace paused. 'Often the consequences aren't what they expect. My elderly mother has a saying: "It rained on the mountain top but it was the valley below that got flooded."'

'Mama would have said something like that as well.' Once again, the words were out before Sade had thought about them.

'You still miss her very much, don't you?' Mrs Wallace said softly. 'Your papa has told me a lot about her. How she always managed to stay calm while he was writing articles that could land him in prison. She must have been a wonderful person.'

Sade felt Mrs Wallace lightly squeeze her arm. They continued their journey to the shops without further talk. How astonishing, she thought, to be walking arm in arm with the woman she had so deeply resented for coming between her and Papa.

The mist had risen by the time they were walking back. The sun warmed the street in dappled patches of light beneath the autumn leaves. Sade took courage to ask a personal question.

'Are you going back to Freetown –?' She broke off. It would take a while before the words 'Mami Cynthie' came naturally.

Papa still listened to the World Service daily on his little radio, even at the Kings' house. The latest news was horrible. Sade had heard Papa tell Aunt Gracie that seventy people had been killed fleeing from Freetown when their truck overturned. They had been escaping from Nigerian bombs.

'I think about it – all the time.' Mrs Wallace hesitated. Sade was aware that it took an effort to answer the question. 'My family say I mustn't come. My editor has just been arrested. My brother says he is doing everything he can to find Edward. My heart wants me to go – but my head tells me to stay.'

Her voice trembled slightly but she continued, telling Sade that President Kabbah was coming to London for a conference on Sierra Leone.

'I'm going to attend it, Sade! I want them to hear about Edward. They must consider the children. They mustn't just talk about putting Kabbah back in power. They must think deeper. All our children see is fighting and war. When we, the adults, finally make peace, what will we do with our children who have learned our violence?'

Sade heard the pain, passion and anger as Mrs Wallace's voice rose. Suddenly it fell.

'How will they learn to play again ... become ordinary children again? They are our future.'

The words touched Sade. She didn't know how to reply, except that it felt right to slip her arm through Mami Cynthie's.

CHAPTER 35

'Bury truth in the thickest coffin . . .'

They didn't go to Gary's house after all. Gary had sensed that Femi just wanted to go back to his family. Even so, Femi dreaded speaking to Papa. He was relieved when Gary agreed to spend the rest of the morning at the Kings', playing Ayo in his room. It was the first time that Femi had shown Gary the little wooden board with the smooth blue-brown pebbles. Sade had saved it for him twice now. She had packed it into his rucksack that awful day when they had fled from their home in Lagos. This second time she had packed it, along with the family photo, in the bag that she had brought for him to Aunt Gracie's.

After Femi had explained the rules to Gary, they played mostly in silence. Gary didn't press Femi with questions about the future that he couldn't have answered anyway. If Papa was going to send him to Uncle Dele, this might be the last time he would see Gary. He didn't want to think about it. As he watched Gary click the gate shut, each called out, 'See you!'

Femi could hear Papa in the living room with Aunt Gracie, Uncle Roy and Mrs Wallace. He wavered.

Should he run right in and beg Papa's forgiveness? But he couldn't bring himself to do it in front of everyone. He needed Papa on his own. So he slunk back upstairs. At lunchtime, Aunt Gracie called him down to have some of Mrs Wallace's red pepper soup. Papa hardly seemed to notice him. The mood around the table was sombre and Uncle Roy made none of his usual jokes. Afterwards, Femi escaped back to his comics. If Papa would only come up to his room, at least he could face him in private. Later, Mrs Wallace put her head round his door to say goodbye. Papa was taking her back to her lodgings. Femi heard them going out. Usually Papa came to say where he was going. Today he was probably too furious.

Femi buried himself in playing with his Gameboy. It had been a present from Papa for his twelfth birthday. When he heard soft knocking at his door, he expected to hear Aunt Gracie's voice. Instead it was Sade. His first instinct was to ignore her, like she had done to him this morning. Those charred, dead pieces of wood seemed to mean more to her than he did. He heard the handle turning. Unless he jumped up and slammed the door in her face, she was coming in. Bending over his Gameboy, he pretended not to hear her.

'Femi, we've got to talk.' She sounded more worried than furious. He ducked his head further as she perched herself at the end of his bed.

'I'm sorry I've been so mad at you, Femi. You're not the only one who has made mistakes. I tried to warn you about that Errol Richards, but I didn't tell you properly.' She paused. 'I didn't tell you why I called him Lizard Eyes.'

Femi's fingers paused over the Gameboy.

'If I'd told you everything, maybe you'd have believed me when I said to keep away.'

'Told me what?' he mumbled.

'It was too – too disgusting.' His sister's voice sank to just above a whisper. 'I never told anyone. He made me feel so ashamed.'

Femi raised his head enough to see Sade's hands clenched so tightly that her knuckles were pale.

'He caught me at school – last year – on a Friday afternoon when there was no one there – except him and his friend. I couldn't do anything –' Her voice snagged, then broke in a deluge. 'He and his friend pushed me against the wall, and he was saying all these stupid things, like I was an "African Queen", and his tongue was flicking all over my face and his hand crawling all over me and I was struggling to get away and all the time he was watching me like a lizard –'

'I'd have killed him!' Femi broke in. 'Papa could have killed him! Why didn't you tell, Sade?'

'I was too shocked. Maybe if Mama was alive, I could have told her. All weekend I kept thinking what I should do. I wanted to tell Papa but I didn't know how – and he was busy. I was really scared that Lizard Eyes would get me again. But on Monday he wasn't in school! They'd caught him dealing. That's when he got expelled and sent away. So I pushed him out of my mind. I tried to bury everything.'

They were both silent. Femi understood about burying things that hurt. He also knew how they could wash up. A picture flashed into his head of a commotion on Leki Beach. Mama had stopped them running with the crowd to the edge of the water. She had insisted they leave, but they had already glimpsed the bloated body. What was it that she had said?

'Bury truth in the thickest coffin under the sea and it will break open.'

The words emerged in his head as clear and candid as if Mama were standing beside him now. He wondered if Sade remembered too. But as his mind flicked back to the nasty picture of his sister trapped by two boys, there was something more pressing.

'Who was the boy with Errol? Was it James?' he asked nervously.

Sade shook her head. 'He was a white boy. He's not in school any more.'

Femi felt a small leap of relief but said nothing. His sister stood up to leave, no longer looking so tense but still miserable. Femi leant over his bed and pulled out his Ayo board from underneath.

'Do you want a game?' he asked tentatively.

'I've forgotten how to play.'

'You can't have, Sade!'

His protest forced a fleeting smile and she sat down again.

When Papa entered the room, they were still cross-legged on the carpet, hunched over the board. His father's eyes weren't as blazing as Femi feared, just deeply weary.

'I've got one piece of good news. The police have got Errol Richards and charged him.'

'They've got Errol?' Femi jumped to his feet, accidentally kicking the Ayo board and sending the pebbles flying.

'How, Papa? How do they know it was him?' Sade was incredulous.

'Come downstairs and I'll tell you. Your uncle and auntie will also want to hear this.'

Aunt Gracie insisted that Papa sit down in an armchair with a cup of tea before he could begin.

'You look worn out,' she said. 'We can wait while you gather your breath.'

Femi wanted to say that he couldn't wait, but he held his tongue. Papa took a couple of sips and began.

After taking Mami Cynthie home, he had called in at the police station, expecting to be told there were no new developments. Instead, the sergeant told him that they had received a call from a tenant in their block of flats. The man had noticed a petrol can in one of the large rubbish bins. It seemed too obvious a place for anyone to leave evidence, but he had called the police anyway to check the fingerprints. They were Errol's! The police had lost no time in arresting and charging him with arson and being 'reckless to endanger life'.

'Reckless to endanger life?' Femi's voice rose. 'Is that like murder?'

'Not quite as bad as murder, but it's very serious.'

'Will they let him out on bail?' Sade asked.

'I hope not,' Papa said adamantly. 'But we can't be sure until it goes to court. The sergeant says they will oppose bail so he can't interfere with the witnesses.'

'Who are the witnesses, Papa?' Femi screwed up his face.

'We are, I assume,' said Papa quietly. 'We are.' He lifted his cup and gazed at Femi.

'I'm sorry, Papa,' Femi whispered, lowering his eyes. 'Very sorry.'

CHAPTER 36

A Voice in the Head

Femi remained downstairs. When Papa rang Uncle Dele from the telephone in the hallway, he pulled himself away from the television and sat at the bottom of the stairs. Papa switched from English to Yoruba, speaking so fast and low that Femi couldn't follow at times. It seemed that Uncle Dele was urging them to come immediately. Papa kept talking about the difficulties. His job, Sade's schoolwork, the police and the court case, the Immigration Office, his lawyer ... The one person whom Papa didn't mention was Femi. Did that mean that he was not going to be sent away by himself? In the end, Papa agreed that all three of them would go to Devon in a week's time when it was half-term. He would arrange a few days off work and Sade wouldn't have to miss any school. They could then discuss the future together.

Femi's mind was racing. He didn't want to spend another week like the last one, feeling so miserable and with nothing to do. With Errol out of the way, he should be all right.

'Can I go back to school tomorrow, Papa?' The question sprang out of his mouth as soon as his father replaced the receiver.

Papa's eyebrows shot up. 'Have you thought whether your teachers will want you?'

Femi flushed. How stupid of him. He had been thinking so much about Errol, he had forgotten the rest.

'I went to your school last week. I spoke to Mr Gordon and Ms Hassan.' Femi squirmed under thousands of pins and needles. In addition to everything else, Papa would have found out about the missed Parents' Evening.

'You should count yourself lucky. Ms Hassan seems to like you.' Papa's eyes bored into him. 'They've been investigating who Errol Richards had dealing for him. Last Saturday gave them a good clue –'

'Is James going to be expelled?' Femi burst out.

'James used to be one of Ms Hassan's best students. She also said she doesn't want to see you go down the same road.' Papa hadn't answered his question. Femi tried to pay attention to what Papa was saying about what he expected from him, but his mind was swamped with new worries. If James were expelled, that would be because of what he, Femi, had told the police. Everyone in school would know. James was popular. James would hate him and everyone else would too.

'Are you listening to me, Femi?'

'Yes, Papa.' He tried to sound attentive.

'I want to know that you'll have nothing to do with those boys again.'

'Yes, Papa,' he repeated automatically. But how could he be sure that they would have nothing to do with him?

*

193

With his head tucked under his hood, Femi walked with Sade up the school drive on Monday morning. He only dived away from her when he saw Gary. At registration, he tried not to look at the terminator eyebrows as he handed Ms Hassan a letter from Papa and slipped back to his desk while she read it. He pretended not to hear the 'Hey, Femi!' whispers. He waited nervously for Ms Hassan to say something in front of everyone or, at the least, call him back. However, she carried on with form business and only called Femi aside when everyone was leaving the classroom.

'I'm not going over the past.' Her voice was crisp. 'As your father told you, we are giving you another chance. Don't mess it up. If you've got any problems, come and see me.'

Femi nodded, staring at the neat silver buckle on her belt.

'I expect you to look at me, Femi.'

His head felt as stiff as if it were chained to the ground. It was an effort to push it upwards until her flecked brown eyes fixed him steadily.

'Do you understand what I'm saying?'

He mouthed, 'Yes, miss,' and heard a small sigh before she told him to hurry to his English class.

Gary acted as a shield at break and warded off questioners. They were mainly children from their class and other Year Sevens who lived on the estate and who had seen the burnt-out flat. There was no sign of members of the gang in the playground. Perhaps they were still meeting around the back. He desperately hoped that they were no longer interested in him now that James wasn't there. The siren was ringing when he passed Gul in the corridor. Neither of them stopped but Gul winked. It didn't seem an unfriendly wink.

Femi had even begun to relax a little when, at lunchtime, Dave and Jarrett pushed in next to him in the dinner queue.

'Is it true you got Errol nicked?' Dave demanded. His voice was offhand but his flickering green eyes seemed as if they might strike. Femi shook his head.

'Go on, tell the truth, yeah! We're your mates, man!' Dave persisted.

'Did James get cut up 'cause of you?' Jarrett rested his fingers lightly on Femi's upper arm, ready to close in like handcuffs. He shrugged and pulled his arm away as Gary swiftly squeezed in between him and the two Year Nines.

'Leave him,' said Gary. 'He doesn't want to talk about it.'

'You keep out of this, yeah! Femi's got a tongue,' Dave retorted, shoving his palm towards Gary. The last thing Femi needed was a fight. He had to say something, do something.

'Don't talk to my friend like that!' Femi was surprised at the force of his defiance. People around them were stopping to look. 'You know what, yeah? I don't want to talk about that other stuff!'

Jarrett raised his hands. The gesture reminded Femi of James.

'Hey, hold it, hold it! We don't have beef with you, Femi! No problem, man!'

Femi glanced sideways. A male teacher whom he didn't recognize was striding towards them.

'See you around, little brother!' Jarrett pulled Dave's

arm and ambled off, grinning. The familiar gesture and words mimicking James's manner were a lightning punch that sent his head spinning. The teacher halted, his face caught between a frown and a question.

'You having chips then?' Gary asked extra loudly. 'My mum won't do 'em any more – gone on a diet!'

The teacher turned around and retreated.

'Yeah,' Femi said weakly. He gripped the counter and ordered his chips. He half expected to turn and see a pair of black pupils in a delicate brown web sizing him up. Femi took his plate and followed Gary, past a blur of faces, to an empty table on the far side of the dining hall. Papa and Ms Hassan expected him to make a new start. They were giving him a second chance. He even had Gary acting as a self-appointed body-guard! But none of them could stop the voice in his head.

You trying to forget me, little brother – after I protected you – got stabbed 'cause of you – expelled 'cause of you . . .

It would have been easier to push away if the voice were simply harsh and accusing. There were accusations that he could throw back. Instead, the voice was really rather sad.

In the changing room, Mr Hendy growled at the boys to hurry up. He said nothing to Femi about his absence; but from the tone of his voice when he placed him in a forward position Femi suspected it was a test. The encounter at lunchtime and James's lingering voice had drained him. It wasn't long before Hendy was shouting at him. Feet not fast enough. Eyes not quick enough. Mind not sharp enough. Halfway through the lesson, he switched Femi into defence. Hendy's voice still kept roaring until his ears felt as though they were splitting as much as every bone in his body.

'What are you holding back for? Tackle him! Tackle him!' The sports teacher was unremitting. At the end of the practice he called Femi aside.

'What's wrong with you, boy? You can be fierce as a terrier, but you're fumbling around like a stuffed poodle! Why do you let everyone else walk over you?'

Femi felt a lump in his throat. Hendy seemed to be talking about more than football.

'Yes, sir,' he managed to mumble.

'What's that?' Hendy exploded. Surely everyone must be listening by now. 'In football you have to take control of the ball – strike for your own goal. Same in life, boy. If you don't, someone else will! They'll have you running in another direction. You get me?'

'Yes, sir!' He tried to sound a little more energetic.

'Well, let me see the change by Thursday.' At least Hendy still wanted him to come to the after-school team practice. He had thrown the ball back to him.

CHAPTER 37

A Crazy Plan?

Sade wasn't at the gate. Femi retreated under his anorak to wait for her. He stared through the tunnel of his hood at the wall across the road where Errol usually hung out. The place was as empty as the desert dunes around the silver coupé in the billboard above. Errol had gone and so had his after-school crowd. Mama would have said something about wasps buzzing round for the honey. A memory from way back stirred. He was sitting alone at their kitchen table in Lagos when wasps began swarming around an open pot of jam in front of him. He screamed and Mama came running. She scooped away the jam. The wasps scattered and she chased them out of the door with a towel. He only stopped crying when she lifted him on to her lap and cuddled him.

Femi's stomach tightened. There was so much he had forgotten. No, not forgotten. Buried. It hurt so much to remember Mama. Yet her voice never came accusing him of forgetting her. She let him be.

So why should he let James get inside his head and make him feel guilty? Hadn't James forgotten a few things? Like the first time they met. The awful howl from a teacher whose finger had just been sliced away by a slamming door ... A posse of boys careering around the corner ... James trapping Femi with his camera-eyes ... finding him later in the dining hall ... calling him 'little brother' ... telling him to give Sade a message. If only he had had the courage to tell Flash Gordon what he had seen, there and then, none of the rest might have happened. But he had been scared, then flattered. It felt good being called 'little brother' ... being given twenty pounds.

He could see now that one thing had led to another. It was like accidentally slipping over the edge of the riverbank near Grandma's village. The current was so strong that you would be whirled away immediately into the rapids. Papa had issued many warnings to keep him safe. James had issued warnings simply to scare him. Use him. If James were expelled, that would serve him right. He should be glad if he never saw him again. So why couldn't he just banish him from his head? If he added up all the trouble he had got into because of James, it should be dead easy.

'Let's go, Femi!' His sister's face blocked the end of his hood.

On their way back to the Kings, they had to pass the garage. Even from the other side of the road, Femi felt his heart rate increase as soon as he recognized a couple of young men lounging by the old pumps. He was walking so fast that he was almost running, keeping his head well lowered. He sensed Sade struggling to keep pace but she didn't say to slow down until they had left the garage well behind.

'Do you hate James?' Femi asked as she caught up alongside him. He pulled back his hood to hear her. She didn't answer immediately.

'He's not evil,' she said eventually. 'Just stupid to be Lizard Eyes' friend!'

Sade must think he had been very stupid. Didn't Mama say, 'Your father and sister don't suffer fools gladly'?

He almost didn't ask his next question. She might think him completely crazy. Perhaps he was. But if he didn't have the nerve to say it to her, how could he possibly ask Papa?

'I want to see James. Do you think Papa will take me to the hospital?'

'What?' Her voice was sharp. Stinging. 'What do you want to see him for?'

He didn't know why.

'I hear his voice in my head, Sade! I want to get him out!'

'So how does it help – if you see him?' She was always so logical. Too logical.

'I don't know! But maybe then I'll stop thinking about him.' He knew it didn't make sense, but at least his sister was quiet.

He half expected Papa to explode. Instead, to his surprise, Papa agreed without any argument.

'I've been wanting to see this young man myself,' he added. Femi hadn't bargained with Papa coming. He couldn't tell him not to come.

'I'm coming as well.' Sade's eyes gave nothing away. How come she had changed her mind?

'Why not?' said Papa evenly. 'We'll go as a family. I hope the young man has been doing some serious thinking. His mother is deeply worried about him.'

Papa hadn't said anything before about meeting James's mother! Had he met her at school? Femi eyed his father anxiously. It sounded as if he were intending to come and lecture James! James would think that Femi didn't have the guts to come by himself and had deliberately brought Papa to get at him. Hadn't James complained about his own father lecturing him? That was when he had a father. But it was too late to withdraw.

CHAPTER 38

Maximum Vision

The blood dripping through a tube above a pasty-faced woman and the powerful smell of disinfectant turned Femi's stomach. The woman lay under a white blanket on a trolley in the corridor. It was the second time that day that his mind had flashed back to Mama. The hospital where she had worked smelt the same. The blood looked the same. In Lagos, Mama's patients were nearly all black. But blood was blood. Sluggish and scarlet like over-ripe cherries. Red against the white of the walls, the sheets, the cheeks of the woman. His head reeled. Red like the dark crimson stain on Mama's white uniform that Papa had been unable to stop, kneeling over her in their driveway . . .

Femi felt Papa's hand reach gently around his shoulder. Was Papa also thinking about Mama in here? The warmth of Papa's palm and fingers sent a silent message. Femi was unexpectedly glad that he wasn't alone. It would have been horrible coming in here by himself. A couple of passers-by glanced at them sympathetically. Perhaps they thought father and children were coming to visit a sick relative – perhaps even a mother.

At the entrance to the ward, a nurse pointed out

James's bed at the far end. Femi continued to walk close beside Papa through a ward full of patients and visitors. If James were going to be angry with him, at least he wasn't alone. But to Femi's astonishment, as they approached the bed, it was James who appeared awkward. Even sheepish. Sitting beside him was a woman who looked so like James that she had to be his mother. The same broad forehead under cropped brown curly hair, a square chin and dark eyes. James smiled uncertainly, shifting his gaze across the three of them before coming to rest on Femi.

'Hi!' he said. There was no 'little brother'.

'I – we wanted to see if you – you're OK,' Femi stumbled. 'This is my dad.'

'Yeah, and this is my mum.' James glanced self-consciously at his mother.

'Thank you for coming,' said Mrs Dalton. She directed herself to Papa. 'Thank God, James is mending. He's been arguing with me today so I know he's getting better.' She gave a little laugh but it sounded forced.

'Yeah, I'm doing fine. They say I'm doing fine.' James repeated himself. His voice seemed to have lost its confident bounce.

'That's good,' Papa asserted. 'These things can take time. You had a close shave . . .'

'Yeah, they told me.'

'You were lucky,' Papa said quietly. 'An injury so close to the heart –' He didn't complete his sentence. The words of the doctor who had tried to help Mama rushed into Femi's head.

I am very sorry, Mr Solaja. Your wife had no chance. Straight into the heart.

'I should be very angry with you, James.' Papa

202

gripped the rail at the end of the bed. 'But first I'm going to thank you.'

Femi held his breath.

'You saved my son –' Once again Papa stopped abruptly. The corner of his eye looked dangerously wet. Femi felt a jab of embarrassment.

Papa coughed as if clearing his throat and continued. 'It takes years to nurture a life. Seconds to lose it. When you are a parent – like your mother and I – you will know what I'm talking about.'

James said nothing, his gaze fixed downwards on his white blanket. His mother was nodding in agreement while her eyes travelled between Papa and her son.

'It's the truth,' she said. James still didn't raise his head.

'But –' Papa's voice suddenly rumbled, startlingly vehement. 'You led my son into bad, bad company – led him astray! However, I know there must be some good in you. Otherwise, why did you defend Femi at the last minute?' His hand flung upwards with his question, as if catching the air and shaking it would make James look up. Instead James lowered his head further. Femi had never seen him so uncomfortable. Even when Errol had lost his temper, James had never looked so defenceless and trapped.

'Papa!' Sade's face was as anxious as her whisper. Some patients and other visitors were looking in their direction. The nurse near the entrance appeared to be on the point of coming over. They might be asked to leave!

'I'm sorry. I didn't mean to shout,' said Papa, lowering his voice. 'Excuse me a minute.' He walked away and came back with a chair that he placed beside the bed opposite James's mother. She was supporting her head with her elbow on the armrest and looked very tired. James cast a furtive glance at Papa as he sat down.

'When I was a boy, James, there was a forest behind our village,' Papa began. Femi and Sade edged nearer him. Papa was clearly preparing to stay a while. 'My father warned me never to leave the main path. We used it to walk to school in the neighbouring village. Sometimes a boy called Deji walked with me. He was much bigger and older but he kept failing his exams so they kept him in the same class for three years. He often asked me to help him with his work. I did – but he resented it.

'Well, one day he and I were walking home and a bush rat dashed across the path into the bush. Deji dared me to chase it. I wanted to show him that I wasn't a weakling. So I tore after the bush rat with my sling. I was determined to kill it. I didn't even bother to check if Deji was following me. I was going to show him!' Papa wagged his finger, pausing to take breath.

Femi knew the story, but somehow his father always made it sound fresh. He noticed that James's eyes were also darting up periodically in Papa's direction.

'Well, I got the bush rat, eh! But then I realized that I was totally lost! I shouted to Deji but there was no reply. It was starting to get dark. My mother would begin to worry. As soon as she knew I wasn't with my other school friends, she would tell my father. He had a fierce temper. I knew that Deji would just say that I had run off and nothing about his dare.'

James's eyes were now riveted on Papa.

'My father assembled a team of men to scour the

forest with lamps. He made Deji show them where I had left him on the path. It took them three hours to find me. I had never been so petrified in my life. Every creak and rustle made me imagine the worst. In fact, I was so relieved to be found that I forgot to bring the bush rat!

'I knew I was in for a beating. My father waited until we got home. Then he interrogated me in front of Deji. That boy was panicking, eh! If I told my father about the dare, he would tell Deji's father and he would also get a beating! I decided to say nothing about Deji. Perhaps I was just too worn out. Or maybe it seemed pointless. It wouldn't lessen my beating. It might have even made my father madder that I was trying to blame someone else for what had been my choice.

'My mother begged him to wait until the morning. She must have hoped he would calm down and not beat me so hard. But he was determined to let me feel his anger while it was blazing hot. He took me into a side room where my mother, brothers, sisters and Deji could hear but not see us. I tried not to cry but my father's belt bit me until I was screaming. When he finally stopped, I had to hobble past everyone, with my head hanging down, to get to my bed.

'I could hardly move the next day. My mother wanted to let me stay at home but my father insisted I go to school. When Deji saw me, he looked a little shame-faced. I decided not to say anything to him. To be quite honest, I despised him. I had found out how weak he was – despite his big mouth and muscles.'

Papa had slowly edged himself forward. He drew back now on his chair, folding his arms. Femi nervously sucked in his cheeks. The story was over. Why had

205

Papa told James this long story about Deji? Was he going to begin his lecture now? Instead Papa remained quietly tapping his elbow.

'That Deji was a fool.'

Papa raised his eyebrows, waiting for James to say more, but James looked away.

'Well, I don't think you're a fool,' said Papa. 'What's more, you showed courage – moral courage – when you protected Femi.'

James frowned in surprise.

'But when you covered up the truth – to protect your friend Errol – that was different. That wasn't courage. Loyalty can be misplaced, you know. Your friend is a young man throwing his life away – and taking others with him. What a waste!' Papa's low voice throbbed angrily and he was leaning forward again. 'Another young black man bites the dust. Eh! Eh! The racists must be laughing.'

Femi thought he had seen James's shutters threatening to come down. But now they were wavering, uncertain.

'Are you listening, James? It's what I've been trying to tell you.' His mother sighed.

'When my mother thought I was being short-sighted,' Papa paused to make his point, 'she used to say: "The goat thinks the world is made of bush."'

James pressed his lips together. Femi could tell he didn't know what to make of Papa's stories or how to respond. Papa stood up from the chair and moved away to the end of the bed. He eyed Sade and Femi.

'Is there anything else you want to say before we go?'

Femi panicked. They were leaving already and he had hardly said anything.

'D'you know what Errol did to our flat, man?' he blurted. 'Set it alight! He could have killed us!'

'He's been charged,' Sade added swiftly. 'The police have his fingerprints on the petrol can.' It sounded like she was saying 'I told you so'. James looked uneasy.

'Yeah, well, I don't hear too much in here.'

'Is that all you can say?' Sade was suddenly sharp. 'We tell you that we might all have been dead – and the police think it's your friend Lizard Eyes – and that's all you can say?'

James returned her gaze. His lips were parted as if he were about to speak, but no words were ready.

'Let's go, Papa.' Sade shrugged. Her voice was irritable. In a stroke, Femi understood. His sister still wanted to like James! She had always seemed so dismissive but, actually, she was disappointed.

'Yeah, well, I'm sorry about your flat.' James addressed himself to Papa. 'My mum only just told me before you came in. That's why I was shocked when I saw you. Why come to see me if you reckon my friend tried – tried to kill you?'

'Your friend?' Sade said bitingly. 'He nearly killed you too! Or have you forgotten?'

'He's got a bad temper. It makes him do crazy things sometimes.'

'Like selling drugs?' Sade shot back. 'Stealing? Bullying kids? Forcing himself on whoever he fancies? Even when they tell him to get lost! Just a little fun, yes? Like making girls pregnant? When he doesn't even know what a father should be!' Sade was now gripping the bed rail as Papa had done earlier. She was trembling.

Femi saw Papa stare at Sade, frowning. Not angry.

Concerned. Sade was hinting at what she had revealed to Femi yesterday. There were questions in Papa's eyes.

'Easy, Sade girl, easy.' As Papa put an arm around his daughter, she suddenly crumpled against him. Other people in the ward were glancing across at them again.

'It's time for us to go,' Papa said quietly to James. 'Everyone has to make their own journey. It's not too late to find the right way – your own way – through the forest.'

Femi marvelled at how calmly Papa could talk of journeys and forests. Once again, James seemed to be searching for how to respond. Femi knew the feeling.

'Yeah, well –' He hesitated and ran his hand nervously a couple of times over his head. 'Thanks for coming, yeah, and – like I said – I'm sorry – about your flat and – everything.' The words stumbled out. They were an effort but didn't sound false.

'When you're better, perhaps you'll come and visit us.'

Femi's head spun. Was Papa really inviting James to visit them? Femi watched to see if Sade was going to protest. She had straightened herself next to Papa but remained silent.

'Yeah, right, see you around.' James raised his hands. It was almost his familiar gesture.

Papa said goodbye to Mrs Dalton. She thanked him for coming and repeated how she prayed James would listen to Papa's words. As Femi followed Papa and Sade, he glanced back. James winked and his lips silently mouthed two words: *Little brother*. Femi's hand rose, then he quickly turned away.

With the stir they had caused, Femi was aware of

eyes trailing them. He didn't care. None of them mattered. None of them could take away his sense of relief. There had been no big bust-up! In fact, the opposite. It was a miracle. Papa hadn't been raving mad at James! Sade seemed angrier than Papa. So why had she come to see him then? He didn't understand girls. It also seemed that Papa didn't understand Sade very well. But after her outburst and the way Papa had looked at her, he had the feeling that Papa was going to try. Femi had been so apprehensive about his father coming with him to the hospital. Yet it turned out that Papa somehow understood more about James than he did! Papa made him feel quite proud to be his son.

At the hospital entrance, they stopped at the top of the steps to get their bearings and locate the bus stop. A convoy of red buses and cars nosed their way along the main road. Above them, lights flickered across the night-smothered jungle of shops, offices, blocks of flats, houses, hoardings, parking lots, garages, streets, alleys. Femi's eyes travelled to the billboard above the bus stop opposite the hospital. A silver coupé glinted in the electric lamplight. It was the same sleek machine in the desert on the hoarding outside his school. Imagine being at that wheel! Imagine if he could fly over those sand dunes on to an open, empty road, going wherever he wished.

It's not too late to find the right way – your own way – through the forest.

That's what Papa had said to James. There was still time for him, too. Papa wasn't talking about a real forest. In London there was nothing like the forest behind Family House with its trees hundreds of feet tall

209

and leaves so thickly interwoven that your eyes had to adjust to darkness even at midday. In London, tall buildings blotted out the light, not trees. So it was the idea of a forest that Papa was talking about. Everyone had to make their own journey. He had very nearly got lost. *A close shave.* Papa could have said that about him too. The problem was that the forest was still all around him. He needed to keep his eyes open wide.

As they walked down the steps, Femi pulled up his hood. He was about to tug it forward and sink his head down into the back. His old tortoise act. But he stopped himself. Maximum vision. That should be his new motto. Mr Hendy would approve. He made himself a promise. If they remained in London, he was going to get into Avon's junior football team. Even if they had to go to Uncle Dele in Devon, he would keep the motto. The place was sure to have its own forests.

A double-decker bus clattered past, veering towards the pavement. Femi checked the number to see if it would take them back to their High Street. Aunt Gracie and Uncle Roy would be waiting with a meal. Femi felt a small burst of energy.

'Hurry, Papa! Sade! I'm starving!'

Femi contorted his face, flickered a grin and bounded ahead to join the queue.

Saturday 1st November

11.45 p.m. (Attic, Uncle Dele's cottage in Devon. Not even a sliver of moon.)

> Outside the bedroom window
> Waves plunge against the cliff
> Ceaseless, tireless.

In the night
A storm breaks
Their rhythm changes
Shaking the world
Making small boats tremble.
In the haze-grey morning
Gulls drift on calm currents
Squawking to greet another day.
Outside the bedroom window
Waves plunge against the cliff
Ceaseless, tireless.

Tonight I feel like we are on one of those small trembling boats, Iyawo, in the middle of a raging sea. We could be turned upside down or smashed against rocks. If Mama were here, she would pray. When the sea is calm, it's deceptive. It can wreck you in a minute.

Until this evening, we were having a peaceful half-term week with Uncle Dele. Walking, talking, eating, relaxing together. Even when the sky was thick with clouds, Uncle insisted we dress up warmly and walk along the coast path. Papa teased him that he has become a real English gentleman! So you see, Iyawo, we've even been laughing.

That peace was wrecked with Papa's news after dinner. He has avoided telling Femi and me because it's so upsetting. But tonight he couldn't hide it any longer. A few weeks ago, he found out that almost every Nigerian who has asked the British Government for asylum in the last three years has been turned down!!!! Can you imagine that, Iyawo? I always believed that when the immigration officers studied Papa's case properly, they would understand how we became refugees. They would know he was telling the truth. But if they haven't believed THOUSANDS of other Nigerians, what are <u>our</u> chances??? They claim they are fair but, if you are Nigerian, they don't even care whether your story is true.

211

So now we are not going back to London. Uncle Dele convinced Papa that he must start writing full-time again and make his voice heard. If lots of people get to know Papa through his writing, it won't be so easy for the government to get rid of us quietly. Papa is going to give up his work in London and Uncle will support us until Papa can earn enough. Uncle is younger so it's hard for Papa to accept being dependent on him. But it's our only hope. Uncle Dele is lucky he doesn't have our problem with immigration. The colleges here want him to teach so they always get him a work permit and he doesn't have to report to the police station every month like Papa. Next year he can apply for a residence permit to stay for as long as he likes. Isn't it crazy that Papa is treated so differently?

It feels like a tidal wave has swept over us, Iyawo. After beginning all my exam courses at Avon, I'm back to Square One. On Monday, we have to register at the high school four miles away from Uncle's village. I won't be surprised if Femi and I are the only African children in the whole school . . . probably the only black children. When Papa asked what we thought, Femi said he didn't mind as long as Gary could visit. He's glad to be far away from Lizard Eyes' gang and he has more freedom to roam around here. But I was silent. Then Papa said, 'Events sometimes dictate our choices, Sade. At least we are together, our small family.'

I'm sure he was thinking of Mami Cynthie and Edward. A Peace Accord was signed last week for her country and the rebels are meant to stop fighting and hand back the child soldiers. Papa fears that the agreement will break down but Mami Cynthie is determined to get a flight to Freetown as soon as possible. It's strange how things change, Iyawo, because actually I'm anxious about her myself.

Poor Papa. He has had to cope with everyone else's stress on top of his own. That includes me being mad at him over Mami Cynthie. While we have been walking, we have talked about so many different things. I told Papa my whole story about Lizard Eyes. He said I mustn't blame myself for not telling him earlier because it was also his fault. It's really hard living in London. We were falling apart there.

So I should try to be positive, shouldn't I, Iyawo? I intend wiping Lizard Eyes out of my brain now. If I'm honest, I have been thinking a bit about James. Will he break with Lizard Eyes' friends and try to turn himself around? Mama used to say you can take a horse to water, but you can't make him drink. She actually said it about Femi, although it wasn't really true. She could get Femi to do most things.

Mama would have loved to see Femi racing along the beach this afternoon. He was playing 'Chase' with a little black Scottie that reminded us all of Bonzo. Seeing my little brother laughing and jumping around again made my eyes prickle. Papa and I were walking arm in arm, with the waves lapping near our feet and fresh salt air blowing into our faces. Papa's eyes looked a bit wet as well. I thought it was the sharp wind but now I realize he must have been thinking about how to break his news. He could have tried to cover up by saying that we had to stay in Devon to keep Femi away from trouble. Instead he was honest with us about our situation. I'm glad. I'd rather face the harsh truth than be tangled in another web of lies.

Well, they haven't deported us yet! Uncle reminded us that Ashanti people say: 'No one knows the story of tomorrow's dawn.'

So we shall steer our little boat to the shore and ... here's my own saying (even if there aren't lots of palm trees in Devon): 'If you have to climb a palm tree, there's no point sitting at the bottom of the trunk, is there?'

AUTHOR'S NOTE

As in *The Other Side of Truth*, my characters are all fictional but there are references to real people and events.

In 1997, the year in which *Web of Lies* is set, General Abacha was still in charge of Nigeria. He had seized power four years earlier and anyone who criticized him and his soldiers was in danger of being arrested, tortured, even executed. Outspoken journalists (like Papa) were a particular target. By 1997, almost 15,000 Nigerians had come to Britain, asking for asylum. Fewer than 25 had been granted permission to stay – and some of those for a limited time only. Many asylum-seekers were left waiting in fear about their future. After Abacha died suddenly in 1998, Nigeria held democratic elections and the country returned to civilian rule.

In Sierra Leone, by 1997 a civil war had been waging for almost six years. When President Kabbah was elected to power and called for a ceasefire in 1996, there were only fragile hopes for peace. Different groups, some with foreign support, fought to control the country's gold and diamonds. Children as young as ten were captured and forced to become child soldiers, mostly by rebel forces; but they were also recruited by units of the Sierra Leonean army. Boys were drugged and taught to kill. Some went on to form their own teenage militias such as the West Side Boys. Freetown, the capital, became the only safe area. In May 1997, Major Johnny Koroma, a soldier in the Sierra Leone army, seized power from President Kabbah and his elected government. Koroma took control of the army and was also supported by some of the rebels, including the West Side Boys. Thousands of educated people fled the country, and others who happened to be overseas (like Papa's friend, Mami Cynthie) found themselves unable to return. The United Nations imposed sanctions and a West African peacekeeping force, led by Nigerian troops, was sent to enforce them.

On 20 October 1997, a Commonwealth conference was held in London to help President Kabbah return to power. (This is the conference that Mami Cynthie tells Sade she is going to attend.) Three days later, Koroma and his military junta agreed to a peace plan that would include child soldiers being handed back to their families. (This is why Mami Cynthie thinks she will be able to return home.) But the agreement was weak and broke down (as Papa feared). Although President Kabbah was restored to government in February 1998, the bitter fighting continued and, by the time peace finally came, many more lives had been lost.

UNICEF estimated than 5,000 children were turned into child soldiers. A further 5,000 were made to carry goods, cook and serve the rebels. In 2003, Sierra Leoneans began to tell their painful stories to a Truth and Reconciliation Commission.